Praise for Sandra Scofield

Beyond Deserving
National Book Award finalist and a highly acclaimed novel
of family conflict and the redeeming power of love.
"An intelligent, wickedly observant novel."
—*New York Times Book Review*

Gringa
"Abilene's coming of age is masterfully conveyed through fully
realized, complex characters and situations. . . .
"Gringa succeeds in creating a richly sensory portrait
of a world in exile—not only in a foreign land but within one
woman's own skin." —*New York Times Book Review*

"A gripping portrait of a woman without a life of her own, whose
identity is connected to sex, humiliation,
and danger." —*Kirkus Reviews*

Plain Seeing
Scofield insightfully, and sometimes poignantly, explores a complex
version of female desire and loss.
—*Austin American Statesman*

Few writers capture feelings of yearning and disappointment
as palpably as Scofield." —*Newsday*

Upcoming Fall 2017

The Last Draft:
A Novelist's Guide to Revision (Penguin)

Also by Sandra Scofield

Fiction

Plain Seeing (Harper)

A Chance to See Egypt (HarperCollins)

Opal on Dry Ground (Villard, Random House)

More Than Allies (Plume)

Walking Dunes (Plume)

Beyond Deserving (Plume)

Gringa (Permanent Press)

Memoir

Mysteries of Love and Grief: Reflections on a Plainswoman's Life
(Texas Tech University Press)

Occasions of Sin (WW Norton)

Craft

The Scene Book: A Primer for the Fiction Writer (Penguin)

Swim

Swim

Stories of the Sixties

Sandra Scofield

Wellstone Press

WELLSTONE PRESS
wellstonepress.com
404 Wilson Road, Ashland, Oregon 97520
541.531.0671

Swim

Contents

Oh Baby Oh

S he stands on the side of the road in the chilly morning air waiting for a ride, and she can't get the melody of that song by the Teddy Bears out of her head: *To know know know him is to love love love him.* It was playing in the diner where she drank watery cocoa while she got ready to keep going toward one ocean instead of back to the other. She would rather hum a song with a hard beat, something by Johnny Rivers, maybe, but she has never been able to call up music in her head without prompts.

When the pickup slows, her heart's flutter warns her that this is the real thing, a stranger's offer. She weighs a hundred pounds. She doesn't know why she didn't pack a pocket knife.

The truck isn't new, it's dinged up all over, but it is gleaming clean and something about that bothers her. She opens the door and throws her pack up on the seat; it's not much bigger than most purses. Before she climbs in she says, How far you going? and the driver says, How far you going? with a smirk. And the thing is, she's made it all the way to Kearney, Nebraska, and she doesn't know what to say. Maybe Stockton, where a boy she barely knows just got home from the army, but if she's going that far, she thinks she ought to see the Pacific Ocean, so she says, San Fran', and he says, Hop in, then, with a little laugh.

His name is Sedlet and she says hers is Noreen, which it's not. He says he's a carpenter and she believes him, because he has a big toolbox in the cab behind the seat and his hands are a workman's hands. Also, his dashboard has wooden detailing.

He says, You can ride the whole way with me, if you talk to me. Make it up if you want, but keep me company. He takes a handkerchief out of his pocket and steers with his elbows while he blows his nose.

Like anybody, she has a story, but the truth is tangled the way truth always is and it makes her feel foolish and vulnerable that she hasn't sorted it out. She says she's mostly been a pre-school teacher's aide, another outright lie. She says she never wants children of her own (that much is true), but it's fine to work with them because she can walk away from them at six o'clock and let other people put them to bed. She heard a teacher say that once.

He says he thinks there's plenty of that kind of work in the Bay Area (she makes a mental note of the phrase); they love kids and pets in California. Maybe all he wants really is talk. It is a long way to California and talk's not a lot to ask for a ride, though Sedlet is a type she knows she won't like. There is no logic to her feeling, but that's why it is a feeling and not a reason. It has to do with his coloring (pale, pinkish) and his size (gangly tall), and especially with the shape of his nostrils, and also with the wood trim on the dashboard, which is pretty but also odd.

They go back and forth for a few minutes about the pleasant weather and the flat terrain and she says she's come from
Chicago (where she has actually never been) and he says he's
come from Wisconsin where he helped his newly married
brother build a house. She gets Camus out of her pack and
reads for a little while. It's *The Stranger. L'Étranger* in French.
She is at a part she likes a lot, when the narrator, Meursault,
and his friends Marie and Raymond have gone to the beach
but have not yet encountered the Arabs. The narrator has
mentioned the color of some of their clothes, and also the
cigarette that he is smoking. She wishes she were walking
along behind the characters, watching them stroll into the
events of the day; or maybe walking toward them slowly,
she would divine in Meursault's face a sign of the violence
inside him. Even though she knows what will happen, the
difficulty of the French slows everything down and increases
the tension. She has been through the book twice, slowly, and
has made many vocabulary notes in the margins, but most of
it isn't easy going, so it absorbs her.

La nuit a passé. That is something to hope for.

He glances at the book. She holds it up for him to see the
title so he won't have to ask. If he wanted, she would read aloud.
She is proud of her accent, even though she is still struggling
with comprehension. She gets whatever is literal, but stalls at
nuance. If he asked, she would try to explain why she likes the
book and the language, she would say that she likes feeling
that she has to reach for meaning—she would use that word,
nuance—and that would pass some time in a way that interests
her.

You went to college, did you? he asks.

University of Texas, Austin. She gives him the Longhorn sign with her forefinger and little finger of her right hand, but he doesn't seem to recognize it for what it is. She doesn't say that she didn't graduate.

I thought I heard a little drawl.

Twang, she says.

What's that?

Southerners have drawls. I'm a Texan.

Wish my hands were free to write that down.

She puts the book away in her bag and stares out the window, thinking of food.

He says, So's that what you studied, French?

Speech, she says. *Pas français.*

The window pane is cool against her forehead. She's pretty sure she'll have a headache before long.

He says, Wouldn't think a person had to study speech unless they're foreign.

It comes out like this: —unless *thur forn*. He could stand a course in grammar; she is thinking he isn't the only car on the road to California. She says, I guess you studied a fancy science? Going to be an astronaut? Knowing as the words come out of her mouth that she is in a sorry situation.

I didn't waste my time with college. Apprenticed. I'm a union carpenter, like my dad.

Good for you. Can I take a nap now and dream up something more to say?

You can put your head in my lap.

She gives him a warning look, all bluff.

When he stops for gas, she's surprised to realize that she has been asleep. Her neck is killing her. He suggests she get something to drink and then he'll look for a place to have lunch.

I've got enough for both of us, he says, but she buys six candy bars, all different, and a bottle of Coke.

They have stopped in a small, pretty town, and he finds the park. He has a hand-sewn muslin bag, she has her little rattling paper sack. They sit across from one another at a picnic table. His larder consists of various kinds of raw nuts, crackers, a tin of pickled beets, a couple of apples and a jar of water. She eats a Baby Ruth and a Tootsie Roll and drinks the Coke. He eats everything he has in a methodical, attentive manner, although he says she can have any of it she wants. She takes one cracker. It looks as if it has been run over. In her entire life she has never had a cracker that wasn't a Saltine. This one tastes fishy and has some kind of seeds that catch between her teeth.

Your skin is spotty because of what you are eating, you know, he says. People don't stop to think that nutrition is the primary basis of our health. Sugar, salt, white flour, fat, meat, chemicals. The American food groups. It's all poison. People get sick. They get acne, headaches, constipation, heart disease, tumors. Kids grow up stunted in every way. He speaks softly, slowly. He is creepy.

She gets up. I need to stretch my legs. If I walk around a few minutes, are you going to leave me behind?

No. I need to stretch, too.

He looks at his watch. He says, Ten minutes, at the truck.

He gathers the trash, including her bottle. I'll get this, he says.

She stomps off into the park, then stomps back toward the truck, keeping an eye on him all the while. From a few yards away she watches him blowing and cleaning out his nose, shaking out the handkerchief, folding it carefully.

As they start down the highway, she takes out her hairbrush and attacks her hair. It feels really good to brush vigorously. Her scalp tingles. Strands fly about.

Sedlet asks her to cut it out. Who knows what's in your hair?

She turns her back to him and cleans her brush, rolls down the window and carefully puts her arm down along the door and lets the detritus go. In her pack, she has a piece of bunched synthetic hair called a "fall" that she can attach to her own hair and now she wishes she was wearing it in a trim little schoolteacher's bun at the nape of her neck. Her hair is growing out from a barber's uneven cut and Sedlet probably thinks it is a reflection of her character.

She naps through the afternoon, leaning against the window. Sedlet is not quite an albino, but his eyelashes are almost white. She wonders how he can work in the sun. He's definitely ugly. He wears his thin hair in a neat pony-tail tied with wound string. She dreams that the hair catches fire, straight up from his head like a torch. It is a pleasant dream.

She knows the day will come when she'll tell about the time she hitch-hiked cross-country, and she won't say how easy it was. To get all the way to Kearney, Nebraska (and Sedlet): two rides and both of them just about walked up and tapped her on the shoulder.

She had been in Feenjon's on MacDougal in the Village in New York City, and she heard a girl whining to her boyfriend. They were going home to Fort Wayne, Indiana in the morning, they were sick to death of New York and their cold water flat.

Someone had broken in the night before while they were on their mattress on the floor, and the intruder, mad that they didn't have anything worth stealing, had peed on them and had pulled the glass doorknob off and taken it with him.

The couple had been in Feenjon's before, chatting up the owner, a Lebanese who had always been nice to her, so she asked him if he would intercede for her about a ride. The next morning she met them at a diner on Broadway in the dark. They had said not to bring too much stuff, but even at that they were surprised when all she carried was a small pack. She has a wallet, a place-setting of her dead mother's silver in a flannel sleeve, the fall of fake hair that matches her own bleached hair, a clean T shirt and underwear, and a dark blue shift with cap sleeves. She's wearing jeans and a long-sleeved blouse and a light jacket. She has about forty dollars she made at a car show in Queens, handing out brochures. And a notebook and the copy of L'Étranger, partly for show, and partly because she has become attached to it for reasons that keep changing.

She was living in a decent studio up on the west side, working Kelly Girl three or four days a week, but her roommate brought home a guy who took up all the breathing space, and besides, she doesn't know how to do anything anyone is buying in New York; she thinks New Yorkers are snippy superior people and she hopes California people give you a little more time to ask or answer a question, at least.

The couple was quarreling, nothing vicious, and she slept off and on the whole way to Indiana. They drove fast and arrived in the middle of the night. She slept on a couch at the girlfriend's parents' house. The next morning over breakfast the girl's mother said she had a good friend who was going to a funeral in Kearney, Nebraska, and she was pretty sure she could go if she could leave right then and if she could help drive. She washed her face, and half an hour later she was in a car as wide as a boat listening to a tubby woman railing against her dead brother who had died in Guatemala of an allergic reaction to mushrooms and had been shipped back, ashes in a can. For all the woman's complaining, *oh it was the perfect death for the sonofabitch, you can bet it was a psycodely mushroom*, she had to pull over on the side of the road outside Ottumwa, howling and farting with grief, too overcome to drive or even ride the rest of the way in. They stopped to sleep a while in a motel—the woman paid—and arrived in Kearney as cars were leaving for the ceremony.

She helped a friendly lady who stayed behind set out casseroles and desserts and then they served themselves huge helpings and put their feet on the furniture and talked about what made a person a wanderer (lack of ambition, no strong attachments; curiosity). The lady, old enough to be somebody's grandmother, said she had never been out of Buffalo County; she seemed to be expecting advice.

When the cars started pulling up in the straggly yard, she went down in the basement to the dead brother's room for the night. There was an upside down American flag on the wall. There was a stack of comic books. She read one, "The Vanishing Ray," about a character called Lady Penelope, and then read "Terror in New York City" before she fell asleep. She wished she had gone to the funeral to see who showed. It would have been interesting to see what the dead man's friends looked like.

In the morning a man in the house gave her a ride to the

highway and pointed the way west, then took her back to a
diner a short walk away. He gave her two dollars and said, We
can always use dependable help in Kearney, you know. Clean
girls who come to work on time. Clerks, secretaries, hospital
help. Those are the girls who can make a life here.

As if.

They stop for dinner at a café. She orders a cheeseburger
and fries with another Coke. Sedlet eats soft boiled eggs and
sliced tomatoes and drinks milk. He pushes himself into the
corner of the booth as if he is getting as far away from her as
he can. If that's so, all he has to do is leave her behind. He's
the one with the keys. She scoots toward the outside of her
seat. Across from her on the wall is a pay phone. She keeps
thinking of calling her grandmother in Wichita Falls:

I want to come home. I'm all alone and it's stupid out here.

My angel. Just come on home.

I've been driving since four in the morning, Noreen. Sedlet
punches her name nastily, as if he has figured her out. I've got
to get some sleep. I'm thinking I'll get a motel about nine. It's
not dark yet, I could take you to a good spot if you want to
hitch a new ride. Or you could stay with me and keep going in
the morning, it's up to you. I expect you don't have any money.

I'm not going to sleep with you. Her plate is clotted with
grease.

You don't have to worry about that. I wouldn't get that close
to you if you paid me. You smell like meat. It's disgusting.

She picks up one of her cold french fries and runs it through
the grease and eats it. She smiles. In that case, I'll take the bird
in hand, Sedlet.

He stops at a crummy cluster of roadside cabins. She goes in and uses the bathroom and brushes her teeth. She tells him she'll sleep in the cab of the truck. He gives her a pillow and the blanket off the bed, leaving him a tacky bedspread. He gives her the key to the truck and a key to the room and says if she needs to come back in she can, but she should knock first because she'll startle him. He seems tired, but he's pleasant, as if they are co-workers on an irksome road trip and she lost a coin flip.

She's sure it will be a long night but before she can work up a thorough fit of self-pity, Sedlet is tapping on the window and she sees the sun is up. She goes inside to take a shower while he heads off and comes back with tea and big dry rolls, and in no time they are on the road again.

They manage for quite a while by naming what they see: the houses along the road. Abandoned vehicles. A little boy sitting on a fence who waves at them. A motionless cow staring over a different fence as if it can't figure out what to do next. They stop at a mom and pop grocery and split the cost of brown bread and cheese, but she won't pay for milk. She hates milk. To please him, she buys orange juice instead of soda pop. She feels the miles behind her and though she is tired to the bone, she is starting to imagine what it is like in California. Growing up in West Texas, she has always liked the idea of living where there are many trees and bodies of water. She closes her eyes and pretends to sleep, but she is seeing little apartments, nothing fancy, not even much of a view, and a café where she sees the same people every day. She doesn't know if she works there or eats there, but people say her name when she comes in.

It only makes sense that the trip will be easier on her if

she keeps Sedlet happy, so that afternoon she tries to think of what she can talk about. Of course: wood.

I know this guy in New York who loves wood. I guess you'd say he has a fetish, if that's the word. He's a cartoonist.

Fetish. Is that a good thing to say about him?

I just mean, he really really loves wood.

Like how? How do you know that?

He has little carvings everywhere in his apartment. Trolls and fertility symbols mostly. And his bathroom. His shower is lined with cedar. His toilet seat is oak. And his toilet tank, too. When you walk into his apartment that's the first thing you notice, the smell of wood.

That doesn't sound fetishy to me.

He's a really famous cartoonist. You'd know who he is. Do you read *Playboy*?

Nope. What's his name?

You probably wouldn't know him then. Never mind.

Did you do him? Is that why you were in his apartment? Is he famous for fucking? Are you?

I went there because there was a snowstorm. We were in Feenjon's in the Village and his apartment was closer than mine. He was being nice.

You didn't answer me.

None of your business.

Sedlet hoots. A fetish, he says, is sexual. A fetish is like he has a wooden dildo he shoves up your vagina. Or he has you shove it up his butt. Was it like that?

She rummages around in her bag and takes out her notebook and a pen. She scribbles furiously.

What are you writing?

You don't need to know. It's private.

We're talking about sex and you can't tell me what you're writing?

That's right.

He makes a grab for her notebook but she pulls it away.

Watch the road, Sedlet.

You are turning out to be more entertaining than I thought you would.

I'm so flattered.

What do you write in your notebook?

Stuff. I write down stuff about my life as it is happening. I'll read it to you: Sedlet dash fetish dash wooden dildo.

Hey! It sounds like I'm the one with the fetish!

You'll just have to have faith I'll remember it was a conversation and I won't misrepresent you.

I think you've got a mean streak. Somebody didn't treat you right way back when and it comes out with men. I'm right, aren't I?

You mean you don't think it could be you? When I put my thumb out back there I wanted a ride. I didn't want a lecture on nutrition. I didn't want to talk about sex.

He snorts but he shuts up.

The traffic is thin. They are driving into the sun. Before you know it, it will be night again and where will she be?

I think I better get another ride. I'd rather wait for a town, though, if that's okay with you.

He pats the steering wheel lightly with his fist. Look, I'm not a bad guy. I'm not going to drop you off in the middle of nowhere. You haven't got a lick of sense. I'm going where you're going and even if you don't like me you know I won't

hurt you. I'll get you there in one piece and then you can mess
yourself up however you want. And who knows? Maybe you'll
start a new life in California. I live on Mount Tam. It is a very
spiritual place.

That sounds just fine. What about tonight?

I've been thinking about that. I've got friends who live
more or less on the way. I'm sure they'd put us up.

She turns her back to him and curls up. Let me know when
we're there.

His friends are living in a converted chicken house on
the property of the girl's parents. This is someplace south
of Provo. The chicken house isn't completely converted yet
and his friends are totally unskilled. Even she can see their
haplessness. They need to fix the roof. They have spent weeks
shoveling out shit and propping up the support beams. The
girl's pregnant; she's skinny except for the pouch of her belly.
She touches it every two minutes.

Sedlet volunteers to help.

The parents have a big house, tidy as a convent, with banks
of beautiful flowers, and she can't understand why the couple
doesn't live in that house. There is no sign of the folks except
for a plume of smoke from the kitchen chimney.

They eat bad food that includes wobbly slabs of tofu (new
to her) and slimy greens, and once again she sleeps in the
cab of the truck, this time without a blanket or pillow. The
next morning she helps half-heartedly for a couple of hours,
picking things up and putting them down, but Sedlet tells
her she is useless, and she tromps around the place until she
finds a nice spot to read her book. She is incredibly hungry.

The girl finds her and sits with her and tells her how much she misses the golden light of Marin, where she had found a kind of peace and oneness with God and nature and her friends. She is hoping to go back there and raise her child because people there are making a new world, but she was so sick right when she got pregnant, and she couldn't work and coming home made sense for now, but it's hard, because of her partner not being Mormon. She seems to think that her story is interesting and that she, the visitor, will understand, but what she really thinks is that if the girl's friends were golden like the light in Marin they would have gathered around her while she was sick and expecting and there would have been no need to run home to her Mormon parents' chicken house and bad opinion.

She, the visitor, the hitchhiker, the wanderer, knows that if she wanted, she could live in her grandmother's house as long as she wanted, doing what she wanted. Unfortunately, there is nothing she wants to do in Texas. She has no curiosity about the girl or her predicament. She is getting a migraine. The girl's face isn't all there, that's one of the signs, and there is a pain behind her left eye. She tells the girl these things and alarms her. This works out happily, because the girl runs to the house and back and says that her mother wants her to come up to the house.

The girl's mother says that they don't have any drugs in the house. She seems pleased when she says she doesn't take drugs of any kind; what helps is an ice-pack and a dark room and rest. All that is arranged. She lies down in a room under a comforter and sleeps until dark. She is awakened by the smell of food. In the kitchen she finds the mother washing up from dinner. There is a plate in the oven for her.

She eats slowly, though she is ravenous. It is plain, good

fare, like dinner on a Sunday on her great-grandparents' farm by the Red River. The woman asks her if she is LDS, and she says, No, I'm sorry, I'm not, not knowing what LDS stands for. The woman asks her how long she has known her daughter, and she says she is Sedlet's friend and has just met her daughter who seems like a nice girl.

The woman says, My husband and I don't understand how things are done now. Of course our people crossed great distances in their days, and we send missionaries all over the world. But these crossings are purposeful. Do you understand?

Yes ma'am.

We'll talk when you feel better, if you want. You seem like a serious young woman. I'd be happy to talk with you.

Thank you. I should go out now with the others.

Oh no. You can sleep in here tonight. You can take a hot bath.

Thank you so much. I'd like that.

Is there anyone you would like to call? Someone who would like to know where you are?

My parents are dead, ma'am. I'm not so young, really. I'm used to being on my own.

I see.

I have an education. I'm going to California and I'll get a job there quick enough.

She sees on the woman's face the kind of passive disappointment she knows from her grandmother, who has never really approved of anything she has done since high school, though she is careful not to criticize.

In the morning, Sedlet says the work has gone quickly and they can go on after lunch. He says he will drive until they get there, however long that takes; he doesn't want her to take the wheel. If he gets tired he'll nap now and then, but he wants to get home. He has been away too long. He's missing the mountain. They have no more cross words, not even when she eats the rest of her candy. She thinks his flaky friends have rubbed off on him.

They hardly speak at all.

Sedlet had built his cabin on the mountain. It is set back on a gravel road, a small place. Inside, it is spare to the point of feeling empty, with nothing on the walls, nothing on the surfaces. Everything that can be wood is wood. No wonder he was so touchy about the cartoonist's fetish.

He shows her the toilet and shower. He says there is a sauna outside past the porch. She doesn't know what a sauna is and doesn't ask. He gives her a towel and an itchy blanket and says she can use the futon. That is a new word, too, but it has to be the couch. He tells her that in the morning he will go to the union hall in Marin City to check for work and if there is something for him he will go out on a job and might get back late. She shouldn't worry, she should make herself at home, and when he returns they will talk about what she will do. He sounds like she thinks a kind probation officer might sound, someone who is sure he knows the right thing for you to do and will see to it that you agree.

He goes into the bedroom, which has no door. Across the opening he props a screen made of opaque paper and latticed strips of wood. She can hear him taking off his clothes and easing onto his bed.

She throws herself on the futon, exhausted. It is quite cold in the cabin. She wears her jacket and adjusts the scratchy blanket so that it doesn't touch her bare skin. She sleeps late, rises to find Sedlet gone, showers, and looks for something to eat. She looks in every cabinet and takes an inventory of what she finds, writing it in her notebook: sea salt, oats, soy sauce, brownish rice, two kinds of vinegar, several kinds of roasted seeds, tins and small cloth sacks (like pillowcases) of tea, and a few other items she cannot identify. She puts off eating as long as she can, but finally she boils some of the rice, sprinkles it with salt, and chokes a few bites down. She picks a tea that doesn't smell terrible, but once she brews it, she can't drink it. Even the water tastes bad. She sits down on the futon and bawls. She tries to count the days since she left New York City, but she isn't sure if it has been five or ten. She knows her grandmother has worried about her every one of those days and she resolves to call her as soon as she gets to a telephone—there isn't one in the cabin—and reassure her that she is safe and that she is looking for a job. After that, she feels better. There is always a term of adjustment in a new place.

She goes outside and looks around but she doesn't know what the brush is hiding so she sticks to the gravel, walking up the main road, where she looks both ways and sees no other houses. She stands around for a while but no cars go by. She doesn't know exactly what it should look like or feel like, standing on a mountain road, but this is not it, and whatever Sedlet says, it doesn't feel one bit spiritual, either.

She goes back in the house. She is about crazy trying to think of what she is going to eat, but she tells herself she isn't going to starve in one day. She is angry with herself for gobbling her candy bars in the truck.

She will hear Sedlet's truck on the gravel when he returns, so she opens the cupboards in his bedroom and looks at his things. He has numerous pamphlets and books on weird subjects she has never heard of. Instead of putting them back as she finds them, she turns each one over upside down in a new location, then closes the cupboard. In his closet he has shelves instead of a rod, and his few clothes are neatly folded in rows with narrow aisles between. She moves some of them closer and others farther apart so slightly he probably won't notice. He has a dark blue sweater that might be cashmere. She shakes it out and holds it up. Tissue from its folds falls to the floor. It seems brand new; held to the nose, it smells only of sweater and not of Sedlet. She rolls it into a tight ball and puts it into the bottom of her backpack.

She goes all over the cabin but there isn't anything else to look at, so she tries to sleep some more. She keeps dozing, then waking up startled to find herself in a strange place. Once she thinks she hears peacocks, a sound remembered from the past winter in Mexico.

By the time it is getting dark she is panicky, she is so hungry. She gets her pack and sets out to find someone at home where she can call Nikko Stanidakis in Stockton. The last time she talked to her grandmother, about three weeks ago, her grandmother said that he had called; he had recently been discharged from the army and was eager to contact her. In fact, he had told her grandmother that he wanted to come see her! He had been surprised that her grandmother wasn't sure just where she was. (Reporting this, her grandmother lets her know by the tone of her voice that it bothers her to be left to wonder so often, so long.) He left a phone number, and she has it in her notebook. He will be surprised again, this time to hear that she is so close at hand, and he will come and get her. He is a conventional sort of boy and he will see himself as heroic, though he would say he is only doing what a man does, taking care of a woman in distress, a woman he may be in love with. (She does not yet think of herself and her peers as men and women.)

She has only seen Nikko once, so their relationship is an unlikely one, but that is the way couples meet in movies and books, so why not in real life, too? Love and sex are matters of chance, not reason, and right now there is no reasonable path for her to follow in love or sex or life in general. Who knows? If there were no Nikko out in Stockton, she might have seen something in Sedlet, a mystery worth unraveling, a goodness worth giving up meat and Coca-Cola.

She met Nikko in the spring of 1961, when her speech team from Odessa Junior College went to western regionals on the campus of University of the Pacific in Stockton. The team members were free their last evening and they hung out in a park where there were shiny railroad cars set out for kids to climb on. She had won a medal in a difficult event and was feeling giddy. Nikko was a student at the college out enjoying the balmy weather. He had black hair and black eyes and wore tight jeans and a black T shirt and he looked young and sweet and a little exotic. She was wearing a red flared cotton skirt that swished as she walked, and she had lined her dark eyes with midnight blue pencil. They were standing in line to buy hot dogs and got to talking and decided they weren't hungry after all. She went off with him mostly because she saw one of the team boys, Buzz, watching her, and she wanted him to see her with someone. She was a virgin, and she wanted to do something about it with Buzz. She and Nikko made out, rather innocently, in a caboose. Nikko took down her address and phone number, and he has written her many long letters baring his soul and dreaming up scenarios about their future together. Now, three years and a few weeks later, he is going to save her. The impending scenario is so ridiculous, and so certain, she is cheered up enormously.

It is fairly scary, walking down the mountain road. But this does not seem to be the kind of territory for bears and cats and mountain men, though she has no way of knowing that for sure; and she keeps trudging along until she sees a house and lights.

A large friendly woman answers the door and welcomes her inside. If she is surprised to see a girl wandering along the road in the dark she doesn't show it.

She spills out her story to the woman—her ride from Nebraska with Sedlet, his abandonment of her in his cabin with no food, her wish to contact an old friend—until she has simply run out of steam and the woman can get a word in edgewise.

The woman, Estelle, is plump and tan and strong. They are sitting at a table drinking black tea (oh bliss!) with lots of sugar. Estelle smells of yeast and grass and lavender. She is always smiling. She knows Sedlet, everyone on the road knows each other, she says. He is a good neighbor, a good carpenter, but they are not friends. Estelle says she floats a different river. Behind her, on the wall, there is a photograph of her with another woman. They have their arms on one another's shoulders, they are laughing, they are leaning their heads against one another. So she can guess what river Estelle is on.

Estelle says that she can use her phone to call Stockton and they will talk about the cost when they see how long it takes. No one answers, though. She stares at the phone on its cradle. She had never considered the possibility that he would not be home. Where would he be? She needs him.

Estelle says she was about to make dinner. Do you like spaghetti?

She says she does, although she prefers it white, not brown, and Estelle laughs heartily. She rummages in her cupboard and comes up with packages of pasta in red, purple, orange, and the preferred white. Both of them laugh. The sauce is already made. It is a rich red tomato sauce, with roasted green and red peppers, onions, black olives, and three kinds of cheese. Estelle offers her wine, but she explains about her migraines, and takes water.

She tells Estelle it is the most delicious spaghetti she has ever eaten (though she is not crazy about the olives). She eats until she might get sick. Then she tries Nikko again, but there is no answer. Estelle puts on another kettle of water and talks her into trying Earl Grey tea, which instantly becomes her favorite. Estelle puts on a Rosemary Clooney album and sings along for a while and then gets out another bottle of wine.

She begins talking and can't seem to stop. She tells Estelle about the year she went to Austin to school and fell in with the wrong boys and paid and paid for her bad judgment.

How old are you? Estelle asks. You look about sixteen.

Twenty.

Good grief. You haven't started on your mistakes yet. Your

baby ones don't count. Don't be so hard on yourself.

I've already been so many places, I have to keep a list. I do all the wrong things and then I leave.

You don't have to, Estelle says. Stick around somewhere why don't you.

But no place is ever the right place; I don't know what I'm supposed to do. It's like I'm never really there.

Where are you?

She taps her head, a finger at each temple. Up. Here.

Then she dials the phone and Nikko answers.

Hi, she says. Guess who. My grandmother said you called.

Oh Baby, he says. Oh you sweet girl.

She must remember to tell him she doesn't like that: baby, sweetie, honey, darling. She doesn't like to be called anything at all.

While she waits for Nikko, she washes and dries her hair and pulls it into a little sprig of a ponytail at the nape of her neck. She sits at the kitchen table and Estelle pins on the fall in a figure-eight shaped bun. Estelle gives her makeup to line her eyes and highlight her cheekbones, and she puts on Sedlet's blue sweater.

They settle in the living room, where they are watching Johnny Carson on TV when Nikko arrives. He is wearing jeans, a white T shirt, and a sports coat, and he looks manly and handsome, though he is short. He hugs her exuberantly and he thanks Estelle for "taking care of my girl." Estelle's expression is rare and funny, combining pleasure and skepticism. Nikko has brought her a bottle of ouzo.

She writes Estelle's address and phone number in her

notebook and kisses her goodbye and waves as the car pulls away, although it is so dark she doubts Estelle can see her. Nikko has thought to bring cans of pop and a couple of oranges, napkins, and chocolate bars, in case she is hungry on the trip back to Stockton. He says if she would rather go to a restaurant or a diner, that is fine with him, he wants to do whatever she wants to do, but she says she wants to go to his home and sleep in his bed and wake up safe. At that, his head goes back and his mouth opens wide and he makes a sound that is a cross between a chortle and a gag but also a happy sound, and both of them laugh.

The truth is that although she is relieved to be in Nikko's hands for the time being, and though she is impressed with his courtesy and especially with the speed of his response, and though he is obviously clean and neat and anyone would say he is an attractive young man, and he is an ethnic Greek, so at least he has an interesting identity; and he has lived in Germany, albeit on a United States Army base, she is trying to suppress her feelings about him as an Other. A Them. Because when you think about it, guys are aliens.

It is immediately apparent that his virtues are not the qualities that make a man appealing to her, something she knew all the way cross country but simply did not bother to recollect since she had not admitted she was going to call him. He is a nice guy, the equivalent of a small savings bond. She had to have somewhere to go and with forty dollars (now partially depleted) someone to go to, and in the course of what she now thinks of as her adventures he became her destination.

His letters to her from boot camp and from his several

postings were reasonably literate, and affectionate and dreamy in exactly the way millions of letters by lonely boys have been written to girls back home since forever. She never gave Nikko much encouragement, and she thinks that she was fair in that way, but it was always nice to think that there was this guy out there thinking of her, wishing he could see her again. A couple times a year she replied, but her life was troubled, and she never thought he could understand, let alone offer sympathy. When she wrote, it was more to hear what she was thinking than to share it with him. Usually she tore her letters up as giving too much away. She liked to think of him as her clean slate. She always had in mind that boy in the caboose, the one who didn't try to get in her blouse or tongue her and who said she was the sweetest girl he'd ever met, while she was looking for Buzz Southern over his shoulder. In those odd moments of nostalgia, she was astonished that anyone could have been so off the mark about her, and she wondered how much the appraisal was worth, until she shook off such thinking, disgusted with herself.

He is Greek Catholic and she is Catholic, too, though she hasn't attended church since her mother died, except as a tourist in Mexico. If she were the type of girl who wanted to marry and have some babies, he might be a good prospect. She's sure he has an extended family in Stockton; he has mentioned cousins and businesses whose nature she doesn't recall. But she has never wanted a conventional life. She couldn't say what she wants in a man and she knows she doesn't have much to offer in return. She likes the surprise—the alarm—of meeting someone unlike anyone else she has known, someone unsuitable. She doesn't want to be mistreated, but she doesn't expect to be coddled, either, and she never thinks in terms of a future. If she can't believe in God, how is she supposed to believe in men? Her favorite writers right now are Albert Camus and Andre Gide; her dreams are of the exaltation of the senses and the flesh. As she rides through the California night—is she ever to see it in the light?—she thinks that her flight to the west is a stand-in for the desert treks of another continent; she is not resourceful enough to cross an ocean. She will settle for brushes with men who have been places, men who know things. She has practiced on all kinds of boys, and in Mexico, a man or two. She does not think there is one right person for her or for anyone. She believes, more than anything, in luck, but also in something you could call open-heartedness, a quality she hopes she will recognize if she ever sees it in another human being.

She knows she is overreaching, but she hopes it is because she is young and eventually she will close the gap with experience, reading, and reflection. Mistakes are a form of instruction, aren't they?

How will she ever explain that to Nikko?

He lives in a duplex apartment above a row of garages set back from a busy street. His cousin Bruno has the other apartment. There's a lot of street noise and headlights flash through the blinds of the windows. His bed is neatly made.

He says, Bruno is on night shift. I thought I'd sleep over at his place and let you rest. I work in the morning. He looks at his watch—today. I couldn't get out of it. Then I'm off for the weekend.

Don't be silly. Don't you want to stay with me?

He says, I have to be at work in a few hours.

We could sleep together at least. I'd feel funny by myself. Like I ran you out.

He kisses her forehead. When I'm tired like this, I sleep like a rhino, all humped up and noisy.

Who told you? she asks, but he doesn't get it.

There's breakfast stuff here. My friend Angie is going to pick you up for lunch. You'll like her. You can hang out, rest. I'll be home around six. Okay?

Suddenly she is relieved. He's absolutely right. She doesn't want to seduce him. She doesn't want to be with him at all. She holds her arms out.

I'll be fine.

He embraces her and she kisses him sweetly. She tries to be the girl she was three years ago because she knows he is remembering her and wanting her. She runs her tongue along the serration of his teeth. She kisses his chin and his cheeks and his nose and she whispers, thank you so much. She leads and he follows. She knows he is pleased. She knows he would like to stay, if he didn't think it smacked of one night stand. If he wasn't worrying about being tired at work. He hugs her hard, and she can feel his urge to say something, and she's glad that he suppresses it; that he has the sense to know it's too early.

The truth is they have no history at all. They are on the ultimate blind date. It occurs to her that even back in 1961 he knew that she was the bolder of the two, the one with the say, but he had a fantasy about the perfect girl who would unfold like a flower under the heat of his love, but not too soon.

Angie says that Greeks and Italians want to see if you fit in. How is she with food she hasn't eaten before? Like lamb? In olive oil? She says what you do is fill your plate up with what you know you like, before someone starts giving you what you don't. Angie is Italian. She has known Nikko and Bruno since Catholic grade school. She advises salad and pasticcio. Big-haired and full-lipped, she seems open-hearted and smart in the way of girls who are stuck in their mother's lives but will make the most of it. She offers to lend clothes for job-hunting, a couch for sleeping if things get too close for comfort, and an ear for talking. She says, You are in our country here.

Whatever that means, and however much Angie misinterprets her intentions, she is grateful for her generosity. To pay her back, she tells her a little about her months in Mexico, emphasizing that she lived in an out-of-the-way down-at-the-heels resort hotel owned by an old Revolution-era general's son. She helped out at the desk. She tells about the old geezers and the blue-haired women from the Midwest, and the resident iguana on the rocks by the pool, the size of a stretched-out house cat, and the perfume of the orange groves.

This is the same story she wrote her grandmother, who answered with a postcard and asked how long she would be away. All of it is true, as far as it goes. It leaves out the Chinese manager, padding in the night past the hot mineral pool to her room, wearing a short sarong. It leaves out the handsome rancher who appeared and swept her away from her boredom. As she talks, she can feel the thread of connection to the memories unraveling inside her. What-happened becomes what-I-remember, then what-I-want-you-to-hear, and then turns in on itself like a Mobius strip; what remains is this girl who had adventures, behaved badly, and moved on. Telling sends the experience far back into time, where it belongs, where it does not have to be understood or explained or defended, and neither the past nor the tale seem to be about her.

She can tell that Angie is trying to understand how a girl who goes to Mexico has to cross the country like a vagrant and then arrive on a near-stranger's door in the middle of the night, but she is too nice to pry. Angie has heard Nikko's side of the story for what it is worth, and she can bet she sounds better than she is. She sounds less used and more promising.

She won't let Angie pay for lunch. It's not pride as much as willfulness, and she knows she isn't going to be putting out any money in the days to come. She doesn't have much left, but she will look for work soon. After all, she can type 100 words a minute. She can rebuild her resources and figure out what she wants to do while she and Nikko play out his dream of love.

Back in the apartment she finds a T shirt that says University of the Pacific. She starts to put it on but on second thought she rolls it up and stuffs it into her bag, which is bulging. She washes out her underwear and puts it on a hanger in the bathroom. She changes into one of Nikko's clean white T-shirts and reads Camus a while. She can't concentrate because she wants to decide what to do when Nikko comes through the door after work. She wants to surprise him.

All men have fantasies. One of them is that women have them, too.

It is after seven when he shows up, spanking clean. He went to his mother's house from work, where he showered and changed. She is stir-crazy but she looks up casually, as if to say oh, it's you. He says, Hey, you're not dressed? We're in a little bit of a hurry.

You could have called, she says, and laughs. He looks completely confused. She says, That's what women say when their men come home late. She gets up and puts her arms around his neck and gives him a big wet kiss. She steps forward, pushing him hard with her knees, making him walk backward, until his legs back up against a chair. Sit, she says. Don't move.

She takes off the T shirt and tosses it over her shoulder, poses, twirls, bows. She has draped her dress over the back of another chair, and she puts it on, ties the sweater around her waist for later, slips on her flats, runs a brush through her hair (no fall), puts on lipstick without looking, and presents herself, arms flung out.

He is watching her, of course. He looks almost sad. She crosses to him, hikes up her dress and puts a leg on each side of him and sits on his lap. The thick harsh fabric of his crumpled jeans at his crotch juts uncomfortably into her, but she knows that he is swelling beneath it.

Do you want to? She gropes between herself and his jeans, probing for him.

I don't want to have to hurry, he says, breathless, apologetic.

He puts his hands on her butt and his face against her neck. She thinks it is a good moment requiring no comment or action, and she forgets herself and she likes him. She wants to make him happy, she wants to do something for him, and later on, she will.

They go to a cavernous dark restaurant and sit at a huge booth: she and Nikko, Bruno and a girl with bleached white hair, Angie and a slim, almost elegant man who seems older than the others by a good five years. The hostess knows them; she says, Hi fellas. It is an Italian restaurant, and when the menus are passed around, Angie gives her a wink.

Bruno and Nikko order and ask to be served family style, so she doesn't have to think about what to eat. It arrives in bowls and on platters. They talk about the food, compare it to past meals, the time this, the time that. She takes something of everything but eats little. She is steeling herself for questions, but the meal is over and the plates have been cleared before the blonde asks, You from Texas?

She says she is.

You live on a ranch?

No.

Never?

No.

The girl looks disappointed. She leans back and takes Bruno's arm with both hands, so he won't fly away, maybe.

Nikko says, She's been working in New York City, haven't you, honey?

Bruno says, You don't eat? You want to be so skinny?

She notices that he has large teeth and a sharp angle to his jaw.

Lay off, Nikko says.

She doesn't think Bruno was being mean. She thinks Bruno is aggressive and sexy.

She says, I did Kelly Girl in New York. I couldn't find anything steady.

Nikko squeezes her knee.

Bruno lays bills on the table. I gotta go. He gives his girl a peck. You get a ride, I'm running late.

He puts his hand out to her and surprised, she pulls her hand free from Nikko to take it. It is an awkward angle, an awkward shake. Work, he says. She is so surprised she laughs.

Bummer, she says. She wonders what his job is and she is determined she will never ask.

You come with us, honey, Angie says to Bruno's date.

The waiter offers coffee and spumoni ice cream, but the table breaks up.

In the car, Nikko kisses her.

He asks her if she wants to go someplace else. She says, You know I don't. She has good feelings toward him, but she is thinking about Bruno's big white teeth.

At the apartment, they don't talk. They don't turn on a light. They take off their clothes, not looking at one another. They slip under the sheet. Nikko is clean and sweet. He has his condom all ready. The packet crackles and makes her think of candy.

Once, in a park in Austin, leaning against a tree on a hot September night, she let a blind date pull her skirt up around her waist because the other couple was having sex nearby, and waiting was boring and the blind date was dull and it was too much effort to talk. The four of them walked home together and on the porch the insolent creep said, I can't believe you did a slutty thing like that.

She plays follow the leader. She thinks of herself in that red skirt she had on when she met Nikko. They lie on their sides in the dark. He has his hand on her hip bone. He taps it and says, like every smug observant guy before him: You don't eat, do you? She wants to tell him that appetite is greed; she eats to stay alive and hardly anything tastes good. She would just as soon sleep, but she gives him her attention.

He tells her about that night they met in the park in 1961. He had a girlfriend from high school, working as a bank teller. She was ready to get married. She wanted to be a mother. He was a second semester freshman.

I met you and I knew that there was a wider world, and that made me decide to join the army.

Did you think of staying in the army? Making a career?

I did think about it. But I want to live here. I have lots of family and friends. I want to go to college, have a family. I want to know the same people all my life.

Did you see her when you came home?

She got married and had her baby while I was gone.

Good for her, huh?

Sure.

She slides her hand down to touch him and he recoils.

You don't like that?

I guess I'm shy.

I'm not a stranger now. You can quit being shy.

Okay.

Or do you think I'll hurt you?

I'm definitely not scared.

So you met a girl in a park and you thought, hey, there's more than one in the world. That's no reason to remember my name, let alone write me letters or come collect me when I call.

You were pretty. I could tell you were smart.

Come on.

She remembers herself, skinny and jittery, wanting to be Natalie Wood.

Really. You were here for that contest thing you'd won. You were sort of floating above the lawn. You talked different from girls I knew.

Nickynickynick.

It's a look you had.

Do I still have it?

Sure you do. You know you do.

I was just precocious, it's a damned curse. You believe things about yourself that turn out not to be true. You grow up and all the people who've been working to get smart all along are and you're not. They have a gift and they appreciate it and you had one and dribbled it away.

You're the kind of girl who teaches or writes books or becomes a doctor.

Nikko. You're not listening. I'm not that girl. I haven't been since tenth grade. I'm working on other things now. I didn't do well in college. I didn't care and I didn't try. You've made me up. It's insulting and it's aggravating and it's tedious.

It's because you're alone. You need someone.

You've got the answers, don't you?

You're smarter, but I'm stronger. And you're real sad, Baby. We have to do something about that.

She lies back. Baby. Guys who think they're serious have always liked to play these games with her. Soul-fuckers. The reason you let me fuck you is you haven't got yourself together. You should think more of yourself. The best ones have had steady girlfriends or a wife. They saw her on Wednesdays or in the afternoons. They warned her not to wear perfume. At least an asshole makes it clear he's just meeting her half-way. That he's a taker with a few minutes to spare.

Nikko puts his hand on the ridge of her hip and slides his fingers along the crevice of her pelvis. Oh Baby, oh, he says.

A little while later he says, You could be happy.

Nikko, still beating his drum. He thinks she's good because he wants her to be. He likes the idea of good women because he's ready for one, like his old girlfriend was ready for a baby.

I was thinking, he says. Maybe you could sign up to teach in the fall as a sub.

I didn't graduate. I did all my college in three years. I'm a course short. French, fourth quarter.

You could do that here.

You can't take your last course off-campus. I don't want to be a teacher.

She sighs. Nikko, I don't know what I'm going to do. I don't even want to know. It's just a visit, okay? Her stomach growls loudly. You know what? I'm starving. I couldn't eat around all those people.

He steps over her. Stay right there. I'll scramble you an egg. Does that suit you? An egg?

He brings her the egg on a plate with a pepperoncini. The egg is cooked a little wetter than she likes it, but she digs in. They're both eager to please.

He says, I want you to have fun on your visit. We'll do whatever you want all weekend. Would you like to drive around tomorrow? See the sights, just you and me.

She gives him the pepper and he pops it in his mouth, stem and all.

He hasn't heard a word she said. He thinks he can win her with a good time. He'll be one of those men who sees his buddies twice a week until they all start dying off. His wife and their wives will be best friends. He'll take loads of pictures and hang them crooked on the walls.

He doesn't know to bring her Germany or his childhood, or even the girl who wanted babies. He doesn't know to speak of things that he has lost, and his dreams that are out of reach. Men don't talk about those things, and those things are all that interest her.

On Saturday, she sees Stockton: the seaport, two wineries. The historical society (native plants, tractors). She plays pool badly and laughs loudly. She feels stuck and guilty, like someone on a cheap cruise. They walk around the university campus. He points out the library. He says they have good graduate programs, teacher training. He offers dinner at a fancy place, but she says she'd rather have a hamburger at a drive-in.

When they get home he says, Tell me everywhere you've been, what you've done.

Easy. College to your army. Classes to your marches. Disappointments, mistakes, nothing that matters.

Don't forget New York.

He hasn't heard about Mexico.

I filed pieces of paper, or typed. I changed jobs every week. I lived in one room with a girl who slept all day, was out all night, and always had her share of the rent because her daddy gave it to her. Sundays I went to a museum. Four or five nights a week I went to a café in the Village.

How can you be twenty? he says.

She'll be twenty-one soon. She wonders if they teach the class she needs in the summer. Her grandmother would pay the tuition. Her grandmother would be proud when she graduated.

Exhausted, she falls into bed on her back. It's always easier to say yes than no. If he just won't want her to talk. She licks her fingers and wets herself when his solicitous foreplay fails to arouse her, and he doesn't seem to notice. Sex is like grinding corn. He whispers things close against her neck and she murmurs a few nonsense syllables and feigns sleep. If she's missed anything, it will come around again. She likes to think of herself as a character in a foreign film. French, not Swedish.

Headlights cut through the shabby venetian blinds.

In the morning she wakes up in a panic and stumbles to the bathroom. She knows where she is, but what if she isn't? Her face is puffy and pale, more so on the right. She had been dreaming that she was floating, a corpse in a river, or maybe she is making that up now.

In the morning she says she feels sick. He says there's mass, then lunch at his mother's, and everyone wants to meet her, but she puts a pillow over her head and he leaves and slams the door.

The day is a dull blur. She shakes out the bed covers and remakes it with the sheets turned over, then crawls in and sleeps. She showers and puts on boxer shorts and a shirt from his drawers. She makes a pile of his dirty clothes, going through his pockets and taking out the change and a couple of dollars and putting the money in her bag. She washes and combs out her fall carefully and hangs it over the back of a chair.

He returns before dark hauling paper plates of moussaka and salad, baklava. She moves the food around on the plates, then tosses it in the garbage. Bruno comes over and they turn the TV on low. The guys sit beside her, one on each side. Nikko asks if she is feeling better, and she says she is. He pats her knee. He pats her damned knee. Bruno's hip feels hot against her own.

Her face straight down in the pillow.

He asks her what she's going to do all day.

She's going to watch TV. Sleep. Wash her hair. Why does it matter.

He leaves her money on the end of the bed. He'll see her later.

That evening, she tells him something she read in the *Notebooks* of Camus.

He went to a theatre where they sold lozenges that had messages on them. Questions about love, like 'Will you meet me after the show?' or 'Will you marry me?' and others say the answers like 'I must,' or 'Yes,' or 'Later today.' Or maybe the answers are on the back and you pass them back and forth. But it's like a little game for lovers, and if it means nothing, you joke and make fun, but if you care, you see something in the little candies, don't you? This light-hearted courtship in a packet of candies.

He gives her a blank stare; maybe she messed the whole thing up, told it clumsily. Maybe Nikko is stupid. She doesn't know where she left the *Notebooks* and that bothers her. She thinks of the things she left in the New York apartment and cringes, not because they were valuable, but because it is the first time she has remembered them. A frying pan and a pillow. Her Smith-Corona portable typewriter and winter coat. Books bought from street vendors. If Natalie doesn't want them, she will put them on the street and her things will pass on to needful passersby, not so bad a thing.

Nikko is looking at her in such a way, she looks at herself, sees that she is still in a T shirt and shorts, still disheveled. He is dirty from his construction work.

You shower, she says, and I'll come in to join you in a minute. But when she goes in the bathroom, he steps out.

She dresses in her jeans and the carpenter's sweater.

They join some friends of his at a bar for supper and there's a band. She likes the music, and when some other people start dancing, she jumps up and insists that he dance with her. She's a good dancer. She can have fun with anyone who dances. After a while she is teaching West Texas dance steps to half a dozen people and having a good time, and he isn't glowering at her anymore. She's hot in the sweater and she lifts it away from her torso and flaps it frequently. Once or twice, maybe she lifts it a little high, maybe she shows her breasts, if anyone is looking.

They enter the apartment laughing, singing a little, touching. She whips off her sweater. Her torso is damp with perspiration. She pulls his shirt off and unzips his pants. She steps out of her jeans. The dancing has excited both of them. He's kissing her and pulling her toward the bed. He sits and tugs her to him. She falls to her knees and goes down to him, her mouth open; she hears the sharpness of his breath, feels his belly go rigid. He jerks her onto the bed. Oh, oh, he says. It's annoying.

They're away from the apartment, having something to eat one evening in the middle of the week. There's something she needs to say before his friends catch up with them. She wants to make him feel right about what she wants to do. If she can make it be something he wants, it will be easier for her, too. He doesn't need to know he's making her crazy: the dirty crowded apartment, the daytime TV, his boring friends, the prospect of a dumb job so she can pay her own way, the inevitability of his realizing that he doesn't like her, not even for sex.

I've been thinking about everything you said, Nikko. About what you once thought of me and how it inspired you. And I've been thinking that I've disappointed you because I haven't moved past that, I haven't become someone you thought I would be by now.

She reaches across the little table for his hand but he clasps his beer glass and raises it to drink. I've been thinking that I'm not that far from that girl, not really, I've just been a little undirected. How many twenty year olds know what they want to do with their lives? How many make mistakes and have to live with them? I haven't done anything great big, you know? I haven't got pregnant. I haven't committed any crimes. At least my mistakes don't upset anyone else's apple carts. Nikko? Are you listening?

Yeah, I'm listening. Thinking about my apple cart.

I haven't even been here a week. How put out are you?

I know I won't like what you're going to say.

Sure you will! I'm going to finish my degree. One course, French 202. By August I'll have my BA. I'll be a good, smart, certified girl.

When are you leaving?

I have to call my grandmother to send me some money for a bus ticket.

Of course he could offer to help, but she knows he won't.

No more hitching? he asks.

I don't think so.

There's a big party Friday night. A barbecue. There'll be a Greek band.

I know I'd like that. I love Greek music. You know, my grandmother will probably send me a money order. Then I have to get to Austin, get registered. I'll get some work easy enough.

She touches his wrist. I'll write, I promise.

A plan, she has a plan. Impatience swells up like bile. She's choking on niceness.

The party is in someone's backyard. It could be an Austin frat party. The smell of meat is in the air. There is a pit barbecue with a skewered haunch of lamb above a bed of coals. Nearby, a traditional grill set up for hamburgers and sausages. Kegs, and barrels of iced drinks. People milling around.

She's done her best to look good. Her fall is carefully pinned in a pony tail high on the crown on her head and it helps to hide the worst of her dark roots. It's a hot evening and she wears only her blue shift and sandals. Nikko walks around with her for a little while. He pulls a paper cup of beer for her from a keg and then he says he'll be back, he's going to talk to someone. The next time she looks up she doesn't see him and doesn't care.

She hates parties, but she tries to think of this one as if she were traveling in a foreign country. She doesn't know anyone, and it doesn't matter what anyone thinks. She walks around with a half-smile on her face. Now and then she sees a familiar face, someone she has met with Nikko. These people nod at her, maybe even say hello, but no one is the slightest bit interested in talking to her. She realizes she is looking for Bruno.

He's over by the pit, tending the lamb. She stands nearby, watching. Smoke curls toward her. The band has arrived and the musicians are tuning up. It's late afternoon, the sun hasn't set, and it is hot. She drinks her beer, and as it hits her, so does her awareness of the pain behind her eyes, so sudden and so severe it nearly drops her to her knees.

She must have made a sound, a gasp. Bruno stands up and takes her elbow.

"Are you okay?"

Oh is all she can say.

He leads her away from the smoke, away from the crowd, back of the house and the garage, into the shade of a tree. There are no chairs, but the grass is nice, and he gestures for her to sit.

You have migraines, don't you? he says.

All the time.

My mom has them. I grew up on migraines. Dark rooms, ice packs, tip-toeing.

And you hated her for them?

No, no. Not like that. I felt bad for her. I felt helpless. She'd get this look. You've got it now.

People are always telling me I've got a certain look.

I know something that would help. Wait here.

She really can't talk. She positions herself so that she can lean forward, her head in her hands, closer to the cool grass. The pain is terrible. A headache like this could last five, eight hours. Nikko isn't going to want to take her home. She feels the panic rising in her, and she tells herself to breathe easy, regular breaths; if she gets agitated, if she cries, her head will explode. She will vomit. Sometimes she is hysterical. And there is nothing to do but wait.

Bruno comes back. There's nobody around. Sit up. Slowly.

She does. The whole damned world is like a Seurat painting. You've got a miracle, Bruno? I need one.

Have you ever smoked pot?

Yes. In Mexico.

When you had a headache?

No.

It'll help. He has a fat one rolled. He lights it and takes a puff and passes it to her. At first it burns her lungs, and she coughs and that hurts even worse, but it's good grass. They pass it back and forth a couple of times and then he leaves it with her. In a while she is calmer. He goes away and comes back with a glass of tepid water and a big towel and a small wet one.

Lie down a while. Against the tree. How are you doing?

He helps her arrange the towel to lie on, and then puts the wet one across her eyes.

It still hurts, I just don't care as much.

That's my girl. He pats her hand and sits with her. Maybe he goes away and returns. Maybe he stays. She doesn't know how much time passes.

She takes the cloth off of her eyes and he is sitting there. His edges are fuzzy.

I don't like him. He hates me.

It's a mismatch. But not such a bad thing. A little time lost for you, that's all.

I hoped you would come over from your apartment, but I didn't know how much I wanted you to until just now.

I couldn't. Too bad, huh?

I guess you aren't an asshole.

I'm an asshole all right. Just not that asshole. You rest. I'll be back.

She dozes and then wakes to the sounds of the band and the smell of food. She's starving. She makes her way back to the crowd. She sees Nikko on the far side. He's standing with several people, half-turned away from her. She waves but either he doesn't see her or pretends not to. Someone is starting a line dance, and showing the steps. She watches, then tries them out, dances for a few minutes. The music is sinewy and robust and alluring and jangling all at once. She thinks that if she could dance and close her eyes she would wake up in a place far away.

The line dances are getting more boisterous and there are cries to join. She is caught up by someone who takes her hand and pulls her along. She dances for what seems a long time, until she is soaked with sweat. She staggers away from the dancing and from the crowd and over to the table where plates of lamb were piled. All of the carved meat is gone, but she sees a hunk left on bone, still red and wet. She picks up the bone and gnaws at it, tearing away strings of meat, chewing, spitting out what is to hard to chew, tearing away more and more, dripping grease onto her dress. She is ravenous.

Bruno appears and gently takes the bone away from her,

and wipes her face and hands with a wet napkin, saying things to her, soothing her. She resists him, she says she is hungry, she loves the lamb, Let go! But he says it's better to eat something else, the meat isn't well done, she will get sick.

The music has changed to something with a different rhythm. Indeed, it is all rhythm, it seems to her. A few men are dancing, thrusting their hips, while the others call out, clapping. Bruno pulls her toward them and the two of them are dancing, their hips moving toward and away from one another, circling, once or twice touching. He shows her how to move her knees loosely so that her hips shimmy, and some of the crowd calls a word she doesn't know and she feels happy. When the music pauses, she falls limply against Bruno, her head on his hot chest. She is happy. She wonders, does he love his girlfriend? Is he so loyal to Nikko?

Nikko grabs her arm so hard it will be bruised and jerks her away from Bruno. He says, Do you know what they are saying? That girl of Nikko's is one hot bitch!

Bruno says, Ease up, Nikko, as Nikko shoves her ahead. He turns to say something to Bruno that she doesn't hear, pushes her on to his car, pushes her in. She looks out the window, hoping Bruno is rushing to save her.

Nikko roars back to the apartment. They race up the steps, her following him, begging him to stop. This is crazy! What is wrong with you? Nikko! Stop! Let's talk!

All week you've been the walking dead, he says. Then you get in public, you get where everyone sees what you are.

He stuffs whatever he sees into her bag and he's back down the steps, pulling her, hurting her. At the last step her fall catches on something and is torn off her crown, hurting her scalp. She yelps and he says, That stupid tail! There is no stopping him. She realizes he is throwing her out, throwing her away.

Where are we going?

She thinks: the bus station. There's no way she can call her grandmother now. It's late in Wichita Falls. She would scare her to death. She will have to sit all night and wait for morning to call. It isn't the worst thing. She takes a deep breath. The bus station is okay.

But he doesn't stop in Stockton. He drives on. There's a highway sign: San Francisco.

Where are you going? she shrieks. You're going the wrong way! I want to go to Texas! Stop! Take me back!

She sobs until she is empty. Her head is throbbing. She tries to remember how much money she has. Maybe she can get part of the way toward home, then call her grandmother. She looks at Nikko. What was she thinking? What is she ever thinking?

In a little while, she starts to talk.

Do you think a person must be perfect right from the start? Have you ever heard of mistakes? Forgiveness? What do you want? A robot? A lobotomized idiot girl? That's the only kind of girl who could get along with you! A doll baby. Say something. How can you turn to ice? After three years of romantic fantasy how can you pretend I'm not sitting here hurting? So I didn't work out. I'm not the one. You're not the one. I came a long way. I tried. How can you not care that it's going to be the middle of the night in a big city and I don't have any money? What do you think will happen to me? You have some responsibility here.

He says, I'm taking you back where I got you, on the mountain.

That's idiotic. I don't know those people.

I'm taking you back where I got you, he says again.

Now she's panicking. What is going to happen to her on a mountain in the dark? The first stop light in San Francisco, she leaps out with her bag. As soon as the light changes, Nikko takes off and is gone.

She walks and walks. She finds the bus station. It's mostly dark and empty. She doesn't want to spend the night there. She finds out where to have money sent through Western Union but she can't do that until it is morning. She finds out where there is an all night movie. She puts on her sweater and jacket.

She buys a ticket and goes in to look for a seat. There are maybe a dozen people in the theatre, all men. It smells bad. The movie is in black and white and it is in a foreign language. She never really looks at it. She runs toward the toilets, thinking that she will throw up, but in the hall by the women's toilet she sobs, leaning against the wall.

A young man in a uniform comes to her.

Are you going to be all right, ma'am? he says.

She wipes her eyes. She says, I thought I could watch all the movies all night. I can stay here, can't I?

You aren't supposed to go to sleep. Otherwise it's okay. He speaks with a grave courtesy. She notices the part in his hair, so exact it almost appears to be drawn on.

I wouldn't dare sleep.

I don't think it's a very good place for you. You aren't a prostitute, are you?

No, of course not.

I didn't think you were. You don't have a place to go?

I'm waiting for morning so I can call home for money so I can take a bus to go home. She is crying again. My boyfriend threw me out. Are you about to kick me out? I can't afford a hotel.

No ma'am. Can you come up to the counter? I'm not supposed to leave the counter. I can talk to you there.

I will. I'm going to wash my face first.

In the bathroom, she pulls herself together and washes off the stickiness from meat and sweat. She sees herself in the mirror and takes herself for the joke she is. What did she think was going to happen in Stockton?

She feels caved in, like her chest goes in instead of out. Her legs are wobbly.

At the counter, the young man tells her his name and says she can sit on the stool. He has about forty-five minutes of his shift left. Then he will go to meet his girlfriend, who buses at a nearby diner. They'll go home, and they have a couch where she can spend the night if she wants to. He says he is worried about her. The refreshment stand will close soon and the only theatre personnel will be the projectionist upstairs. And where would she go? This is a big city and she doesn't look like she ought to be out all night. He has lived here all his life and he knows what he is talking about.

She sits on the stool and looks in her bag for her notebook. She says she would like that a lot, if he thinks his girlfriend wouldn't mind. He is a small young man and if he has anything else in mind, she figures she can knock him down with one hard push. He doesn't seem the type.

He says, She is a little slow, and so people don't take the

time to find out what a nice person she is. Do you mind? A retarded person?

Do I mind? Do I mind that you are going to take me, a stranger, into your home for the night? Of course not! I can't believe how kind you are.

For the next half hour she makes notes about the Greek party in her notebook. Then she walks with the young man to the diner and meets his girlfriend, who claps her hands when she hears about their guest.

They live in a nearby railroad apartment that is shabby but neat as a pin. They insist that she sit on their couch while they change out of their uniforms, and they give her a copy of *Readers Digest*. When they have changed, the man finds a radio station with music from the forties, and his girlfriend heats two cans of tomato soup for them. She serves the soup in bowls set on dinner plates, with crackers arranged around the bowls. No one asks questions. When they have finished the soup, the girlfriend gets up and comes back with a saucer on which she has arranged some hard candies, the kind you get at Christmas. After they eat, there are a few chores: the dishes, a little ironing, a sweep-up in front of the stove. They won't let her help, so she goes back to the couch and pretends to read from the magazine.

The girl gives her a pillow and a blanket and a towel. She shakes her hand and wishes her a good night's sleep. She gives her an alarm clock, because she and her boyfriend will sleep in. After she has gone into the bedroom, her boyfriend comes back out. He motions for her to sit, and he sits beside her. He says, I wanted to marry her, but she said it had to be in the church. The priest said he couldn't approve it. He didn't think she knew what she was getting into. We've been together a year. We'll go back and ask again.

She doesn't know what to say. He says that the two of them pray a decade of the Rosary every night. I don't want you to wonder what's going on in there, he says. It's just prayer.

She goes to the bathroom and then lies down on the uncomfortable couch. Something seems to poke her hip, and she rearranges herself numerous times before settling down. Once she is still, she hears the drone, but not the words, of the Hail Marys. Pray for us sinners. She thinks, lucky me to get Catholics, they didn't pull out the Bible. No one has ever tried to save her. She falls asleep.

In the night, she gets up to go to the bathroom. A lot of street light filters into the apartment. The door to the couple's bedroom is ajar. She tiptoes to it and looks inside. They lie crookedly across their bed, their heads on far opposite sides, their arms flung to the edges, but their feet are touching in the middle. The sheet lies across their ankles and the soles of their feet are pale.

Oh, she whispers.

She stands there for a long time, leaning against the hall wall, studying them. She thinks there is something she can learn from them—not now, not tonight, but later, when she looks at her notes and remembers; later, when she knows more and has something to ask the world besides *What next?*

An Easy Pass

Paulo says that I have to move outside the gates to the bunkhouse so the two American stewardesses can have my bedroom. He knows I won't mind; what I mind is that the maids came into my room early this morning and started cleaning, as if I were not still in bed with the heavy drapes drawn shut. When I screamed at them they fled, giggling.

You haven't learned to speak to them, Paulo says. It amuses him that I am intimidated by sullen village girls who swab his tile floors and run feather dusters over the furniture, the banisters, the stuffed animals hanging on the walls. He thinks I should model myself after Ofelia, his secretary, who is bad-tempered and haughty with everyone except him. He says that servants respect a sharp tone and a superior air, and I must practice until I get it right. Both of us know this will not happen.

I am in his room, sitting on his bed yoga-style while he dresses. He has redecorated recently, and the room is made up like one on an African coffee farm, with straw mats and zebra rugs on the floor, crossed spears and a shield on the wall. He moves around in it as if it were a movie set arranged to display him. He is fair-skinned with blond hair and cold blue eyes, narrow-hipped with a compact, powerful torso, and he is fastidious with his clothing. I think he likes me to watch him.

He tosses me a pair of his jeans; we are the same size, 28W-29L. They have worn soft and slightly faded, unsuitable for him but perfect for me. I wriggle out of my own old jeans and into his, then move close to him so that he can feel how well they fit.

Guests will be arriving throughout the day and he tells me that he will be occupied.

Find something to do, he says distractedly, as if I have ever expected him to entertain me. Sometimes he drives me around the ranch in his Land Rover, then takes off in his plane without any explanation, saying that I should move to his hotel if I mind being by myself.

He gives me a swat on my butt that makes me think of my mother sending me out to gather the laundry off the line when I didn't want to do it.

We walk downstairs and out of the huge house along the walkway to his office. An arched wicker trellis above us is festooned with flowers and twisted vines. His hounds run to the edge of the walk and up beside him, panting with love. At the door he says I should come back before lunch. There are some letters in English to be typed, and it would take Ofelia forever. I can do them in no time.

Of course, I say.

I like to be useful, but I will not go in the office if Ofelia is there alone.

Back in my room I see immediately how the maids have put me in my place. Now that I am out of there, they have rearranged the twin beds and brought in a nicer night stand and a big-bellied lamp with a good light. They have folded back the brocaded bedcovers in accordion layers and made the beds with crisp white sheets. Thick towels are arranged like napkins with a fresh bar of soap in the center. I laugh, wondering how the American women will like it when they discover there is no hot water in the bathroom unless they haul it in pans from the kitchen across the hall. Paulo has his own water heater in his room, and there is another in the bedroom they call the Senora's, for Paulo's red-haired mother, where the matador from Mexico City will sleep.

I pull open the top drawer of a huge chest. I intend to take what I need so I won't disturb the guests, but seeing how little there is, I take the drawer and dump it on my bed. I make a pile of everything I own: my old jeans; two T-shirts and a yellow blouse; a skimpy cotton shift; and my underwear and socks. I scoop up one of the towels. I am wearing sandals with soles made from old tires, and I carry my boots. I take everything to the bunkhouse. The dogs are dozing, their back parts on the walk, their heads in the grass. They lift their chins as I pass by, then tuck them again on their paws, and leave me be.

In the bunkhouse I enter a clean, spare room that reminds me of my college boarding house in Austin. There is a woven coverlet on the bed, and on the small bureau are broken artifacts, part of the cache excavated when the bullring was built. There is a flashlight, which I flick on and off immediately to be sure the batteries are good. I listen for anyone else in the building, but it's quiet. There is a room for Paulo's pilot, who uses it for short stays when he does not return with the plane to the capital, where he lives. He is a dark, portly man who always seems vaguely disapproving of everyone except, of course, Paulo. The cook told me that there is a young fighter from Mexico City coming, someone who caught Paulo's eye in a novillada, a kind of practice fight in a minor ring. They will put him out here, too.

I walk to the guardhouse. It is outside the gate by the high stone walls surrounding the house. The walls are topped by spires and gargoyles, like a medieval fortress. I will spend some time until lunch swatting flies and listening to country songs with Milo, the fat guard. The shack is a big room with screened walls and from there Milo sees everything. He is patient with my attempts at Spanish conversation, my endless questions about the way the ranch works and who all the people are who come and go. I have a repertoire of observations that I am able to make about the weather and activities at the ranch, and he comments or asks a few questions, extending my rudimentary language use with new vocabulary or structures, like a tutor. I'm sure he has no idea that he is instructing me. That doesn't mean he likes me, only that he is bored and I am a diversion; that I am friendly and grateful for his company; and maybe the Pátron would want me occupied. I have learned most of my Spanish in this way. I never speak it if Paulo is within hearing distance, but I think it pleases him that I try.

I step carefully. A wild cat is chained near the doorway. It is a jaguarundi, the size of a house cat, related to the panther; it is rare. There is a kind of nasty joke in the way it is chained, as it could not reach the doorway but often terrifies guests. The cat is truly vicious, and Milo feeds it by scooting food—fruit or a freshly-killed rodent—toward it with a long stick. The cat lets Paulo scratch it under the chin as it rubs against his calves. All animals love Paulo.

Milo, with his pistol on his hip, is the main guard (although there is a river to be crossed to reach the ranch from the outside world) but also a kind of receptionist and manager of long distance calls, which often take hours to go through. He has a rickety board with intercom connections to half a dozen rooms and when he has to use it, he scowls and crouches like a bear and sometimes bangs his forehead with the side of his fist.

A parrot, perched on a dowel high in the room, shrieks and startles me. I ask Milo if he has seen Marcelo, and he says that he has gone to the city thirty kilometers away for some supplies. He went very early, Milo says, grinning. I don't catch the humor, but I know it has to do with everyone's amusement that I once had a big crush on Marcelo. Even Paulo reminds me now and then, though Marcelo doesn't speak to me anymore.

The house phone rings and Milo says that the Pátron wants me in his office. He always calls Paulo patron when speaking to others, but in direct address, he calls Paulo Matador. I call Paulo Paulo in all circumstances, most days the only person on hand to say his name.

Ofelia has not arrived; the blinds are still closed and the office has a flickering yellow glow. Paulo pulls me into the room, pushes me against the wall and presses against me.

I'm going to be so busy later, he says. He grins boyishly and shoves his hand hard between my legs. I hear Ofelia's heels clacking along the walk and onto the step on the other side of the door where we are standing, and I pull away with a shy whimper. She comes in with her usual officious air and greets him without a glance my way, then goes into the second room. We can hear her stomping around pulling blinds and turning on machines.

Paulo walks to his desk and pats it with the tips of his fingers. He has only been filling time until Ofelia came, and he says nothing about my retreat from him. I amuse him but I don't think I am desirable to him, only proximate. Sex is like cracking his knuckles.

Then he says that he expects me to come to meals. His friend Felix is coming, and I say I look forward to seeing him again. Felix is an engineer, an intelligent, sweet-tempered man, though I have seen him play macho with the big boys more than once. Paulo has already told me that his movie-star girlfriend Carla is coming from the capital, too, and I think he is warning me to stay out of the way; or maybe he wants me to be with Felix, who has a penis the length of his thumb.

Paulo says I can come to watch the testing of the cows at the ring, of course, but in the evening, after Marcelo and Leonardo entertain the guests with music in the bar, and I have a beer and play cards with the other girls if I want to, I am to go to my room in the bunkhouse for the night.

I am not invited to the orgies.

Paulo has arranged for his plane to transport his guest of honor—a matador from Mexico named Lara—and the girl-friend. I hear the approach of the plane around eleven, and I walk down the road that leads to the runway, past the pasture of the Brahma bulls, past the short path that leads to a dense forest thicket deliberately kept uncleared but contained like an English maze. As the plane is landing I hear the Land Rover behind me, and I step out of the way to let it pass, but Paulo slows down and motions me to hop in the back. I stay in the vehicle as he gets out to greet his guests. A ranch hand has arrived before us in a Jeep to pick up the pilot and the luggage; he has placed steps at the plane's door. Lara steps out and then turns to help a woman who is wearing a beautiful pistachio green linen dress and strappy high heels. She sees Paulo and puts her fingers to her lips and blows him a kiss. So this is Carla. Paulo took her with him to Kenya and Bechuanaland on safari. I have seen photographs on his dresser of her wearing her crisp safari khakis, her hair in pigtails.

He kisses her on her cheek. We are cozy, the four of us. Carla squeezes in beside me and gives me an actress's well-practiced smile. The matador greets me formally and we shake hands; he obviously does not remember meeting me just last week in Acapulco, in the box at the bullring where I sat with Paulo's friends to watch Paulo's wildly successful fight.

We wait until the Jeep zips past us. That driver will unload, then go to the commercial airport near the village to pick up Felix and a girl we all know, Rosie, and the American women whom Felix has invited on Paulo's behalf.

An hour later, we are all gathered in the hall outside the kitchen, sitting on long leather benches under mounted heads of African beasts. There are two American women—pretty, and younger than I expected, and overly made up for the hot countryside, but not cheap looking. They are excited to be on the ranch for what they understand is a special, if mysterious, occasion. I think that they are a cliché, stewardesses and pickups, but I swallow my disdain, imagining what they think of me in turn.

There is an informal lunch buffet. Paulo, Carla and Lara eat in the dining room; the rest of us eat on our laps or from TV trays. Paulo is the first to leave, and he mentions that he will work his horses in the riding ring at six; dinner is at eight. In a matter of moments, the halls are empty as guests are shown to their rooms, except for Rosie, who stays behind with me. We sprawl on a couch and try to outdo one another with our sighing. It is an old joke between us: Who is more bored?

You're looking good, chickadee, Rosie says. I tell her she looks good as ever. She is a plump woman, not yet thirty, with curly black hair and rosebud lips. She always wears tight pants, high heels, and frilly blouses. She has known Paulo since he was a boy. She comes from a prominent Mexico family, but she is a party girl and Paulo says she has no future. He says she should start a business, maybe selling copycat designer jeans in the Zona Rosa, or running an elite escort operation. She knows everyone, he says; she could make a fortune.

In a little while Paulo and the matador meet up at the top of the staircase and leave for the countryside. Rosie and I go through the kitchen and sit on the back balcony overlooking the disused swimming pool and a grove of avocados. In the kitchen, the big Indian cook, Santiago, is deftly carving venison into tidy brochettes and shouting at the maids, who are cutting up fruit and vegetables lazily, as they do everything. Rosie says she'd like to stay in my room with me, if I don't mind. There really isn't anyplace else for her unless they set something up with the stewardesses. I tell her they have my room and I am in the bunkhouse with the pilot, and she says, Ooh, threesies, all the better.

I'll try not to wake you when I come in, she says, laughing at me, but not meanly. She is always frank and often vulgar; I like her a lot. She kisses my cheek and nibbles my earlobe, then tells me I am Paulo's pet, and I say that there are worst things I could be.

Besides, I say, I'm not staying much longer. I say, I've come from somewhere, and I am going back.

The apprentice bullfighter Chule did indeed arrive the night before by bus. When Rosie and I walk to the bunkhouse I see him skirting the back of the building, cutting across to the riding arena. Rosie says she got up hours before her usual time and she wants a nap, so I leave her and go to look for Chule.

Heavy foliage shadows much of the arena. I slide quietly along the red stone tiers and sit several steps up at a good angle to watch. Chule is working a phantom bull, practicing attitude more than skill. This isn't something new to me. Marcelo is part of Paulo's bullfighting retinue, and half a year ago, when we were friends, he showed me fancy passes he never got a chance to use in a ring. He pretended to teach me a few of them, all of it foreplay. He looks like Jean Paul Belmondo, forty pounds heavier.

The young man in the arena is small and ugly, but looks did not keep the Spaniard Juan Belmonte from becoming a great and famous matador half a century ago, and for that matter, Lara is not a handsome man, either, though his bearing is beautiful.

Chule stands like a statue in the sand, calling huh, huh! and

I let myself hear the snort of the bull as Chule is surely doing. After all, I am always saying of my life's perplexities: at least it's something to write about.

I understand that a person sometimes rehearses what he would like to be.

Chule leads his bull with the cape, swinging his arms low. He pulls his chest high, the better to let the beast go by only hairs away. He steps forward and sights the animal again, this time leading with his left hand, across his own body. He passes with a slow sculptured gesture, twisting his body. I go down to the edge of the ring. He swings the cape around again and walks away haughtily, turns and raises his head, smiling. He has bad teeth.

He sees that I have caught him in his play. I call, Hello! as if I have only just arrived, because I know that will make it easier for him, and I see immediately that there is no reason I would want him. He is a boy, maybe eighteen years old. A country boy.

I am all of twenty.

I know who you are, I say. I speak my simple Spanish and offer him my hand. He takes it lightly.

I am sorry, I don't know English.

So speak Spanish, but not too fast.

He looks around, all his pretend arrogance gone. I want to assure him that I would not have approached him in front of anyone. I think of Marcelo and long bitter stories he has told me about matadors: Fags and hipsters, he says, men with flat feet and swollen heads who lost their balls in drink and women. Except Paulo, of course, his bread and butter and, I think, the object of his love.

Everyone is inside, I say.

I know what he is thinking, that I am a gringa, a fool, and worse, the matador's fool, and he has no idea what would be rude and what would not. He has no interest in girls, he is focused only on his training. He is probably a virgin.

The matadors are at the bullring, I say. Could I try? I know a little.

He says the cape is heavier than it looks and it is hot now, with no breeze, but I take it from him. I jerk the cape up and swing it around to the side, and, suddenly embarrassed, I say—what else?—Olé.

He shows me how to stand and how to use the cape to lead the bull out safely away from my body. I don't need the flourish, he tells me, only a flick of the cloth as the animal passes. He says it is enough to know the adorno and to do it well. I know that the adorno is an easy pass with little risk. Little boys use it with calves the size of dogs, and apprentice bullfighters use it when they are afraid.

That way, the toro won't butt you or stick you, he says.

I drop the cape along my leg and I bring my other hand up to my mouth. I laugh nervously.

I didn't mean I was going to do it, I say. I don't think Paulo would let me.

The look he gives me is transparent and tinged with contempt. He doesn't understand what I am doing if it does not matter. He knows he is a boy, and he knows I am not seducing him. Why, then, would I want to practice passes, except to go into the ring with the cows, mothers of the brave toros, as he will? As Marcelo will, and Leonardo, and maybe even Felix, who last year lost the seat of his pants in just that way. The tienta is a serious event and I am a frivolous girl.

My heart is thudding.

Please show me again, I say. I try to be firm but courteous.

He pretends to be the bull. I hold the cape out, and he bends over, his hands up by his head, his index fingers the tips of horns, and he runs by me. I am clumsy and I stop short. He turns sharply and comes back at me. I don't have time to make an adjustment. My right foot is still forward, but I have to lean to the left. He slams against my hip and I fall. One of my sandals flips off my foot.

I sit in the dust and put my shoe back on. There is a second when Chule might have apologized—here he is, knocking the matador's gringa into the dust!—but I'm neither hurt nor angry and he sees that and helps me to my feet.

You are able to try again? he says.

We work maybe half an hour, and then we hear the sound of the Land Rover, and without a word, I leave the arena. He follows me into the bunkhouse and goes to a tiny room, an old storage closet with a cot and one small window high on the wall. In my own room, Rosie is on the bed, snoring softly. I wash my face and hands and leave.

The main room of the bunkhouse smells faintly of formaldehyde. It holds a pool table and a ping pong table and some folding chairs at one end. The long windowless wall is crowded with stuffed creatures that were killed by the boy Paulo. There are many heads of small deer, and carcasses, skins, and heads of other animals, too: porcupine, squirrel, puma, snakes, vultures; and, from farther places, an ocelot and a huge fish on a board. I stand a few steps away from Chule's door, facing the trophies, and practice my simple pass again and again, just clearing the edge of the pool table, until I hear men outside readying the horses for Paulo's evening ride.

Paulo fights from horseback, like the Portuguese, except that in Portugal and in some parts of France, they play the bull but they do not kill it. He told me once that when he was a boy and a bad student in military school in Texas, his father threw up his hands in despair and sent him abroad to the ranch of a Portuguese friend. Paulo came to love that man and his ranch, and more, to love Lusitano horses, which he would go on to breed for his own line. He loved the drama and beauty of the Portuguese corrida, and he mastered it, as he mastered anything he chose, including six languages.

How he trains his beautiful horses could mean their lives or deaths or his own, and every afternoon, he works them intensely while his little wild forest pig, Trini, chases after him, round and round the ring. Today Paulo wears a silver sweat suit of a metallic fabric that looks like tinfoil. He looks like an astronaut.

Everyone comes to watch. The American girls ooh and aah until Felix whispers to them and they stop. When Paulo is done, his men lead the horses away and he comes out of the arena. He unzips the silver suit and steps out of it; sweat cascades off his body. Someone hands him a towel and a clean T-shirt and then he sits on a bench in the shade. He scratches Trini's bristly back with a stick and he claps his hands for someone to bring beer for the men. Trini stands at his feet like a waiting dog until he gives her a kick in the rump and she trots away.

Rosie and I take the two girls by their arms and lead them to the house.

The house has two stories, with balconies all around the second floor, and verandas along one side below. The ranch, a huge tract hacked out over years from low-lying brush and jungle, came to Paulo's father as spoils from the Revolution; the old man, a general, was a founding member of Mexico's monopolistic political party, the PRI. He had the house built on a grand scale and filled the bedrooms and dining room with massive furniture. The couches in the parlors downstairs are from the fifties, made of padded vinyl and laminated wood. The only truly modern room is the kitchen, equipped like a restaurant. The walls throughout the house are hung with mirrors, masks, and trophy animals, and a few bad paintings. Upstairs, I open the door to the library to show the women stools made of elephant feet. Downstairs they look at tiger paw ashtrays and a standing polar bear whose massive front paws are fixed in a furious, menacing gesture. The women are beginning to look slightly drunk.

Usually there are a couple of archeologists around, I say, but they don't much like parties.

Solemn buggers, Rosie says.

I show the women the locked cupboard that holds hundreds of artifacts dug up when Paulo had the bullring built. I explain that the government of Mexico owns all such finds and requires the presence of the archeologists, but they leave these trifles behind for cataloguing at some future time. If ever. I can see that the women have no interest in archeology.

And here's the hot tub, you'll love it late at night, Rosie says. No suits allowed.

The hot tub is just outside Marcelo's room, and I can hear his radio playing awful ranch ballads. I say there is more to see but it is more of the same. I wonder what they would think if they looked in the crates in the cupboard beneath the stairs, where Paulo stores military guns. Or in the bottom drawers of the cabinets in his office, where he files the pornographic photographs he receives by subscription from Sweden.

Rosie says we should go back to the bunkhouse; we have nothing else to do until dinner. I remember the letters I am supposed to type but I tell myself it is better for me to act as hostess to these women to whom no attention will be paid until late at night. I get Cokes for us from an upstairs refrigerator and we stride past the men who are still hanging around the arena.

I suggest we look at the stables, a beautiful building completely lined in white and blue tiles, but Rosie is impatient to get indoors. She locks the door and motions for everyone to sit on the bed. She unwraps a wad of hashish the size of a lemon from a handkerchief. I say Paulo will kill her if he finds out, and he will take her dope away. I tell the women how Rosie once baked stoner brownies and left them in the kitchen, where the foreman ate some unaware, and she was banned from the ranch for a year. The stewardesses, eyeing the hashish, say they won't say a word to anyone. Rosie lays shavings along a crumbled ridge of marijuana in a cigarette paper, and expertly rolls and lights the packet and draws deeply. We pass it around.

The girls are more experienced than they had first seemed to me. One of them lives in Dallas, and I tease her about her twang, pinning its origins down to some place west of San

Angelo, like me. She admits I'm right but she won't say what town, probably because it is so small and has such a rural name she thinks we will laugh. She says the airline worked with her to make her voice less nasal but told her that they still wanted her to sound Texan, that men find it attractive. She fans her face with her hands and says that she is hot and she takes off her shirt, showing her pretty breasts in a lace-fringed bra. Her friend leans over to adjust a twisted strap and says that she is from California, where nobody has much of an accent unless they come from somewhere else.

The Dallas girl gets up and stands cock-eyed at the end of the bed and gives us a whole spiel about safety and oxygen masks and seat cushions, then crumples like soft cloth back on the bed against me, and I discover that I like her, maybe because she is from West Texas. Before long she starts to cry, and says, Everything is so very sad!

Rosie and I laugh and then all of us march to the women's (my!) room in the house for a bath. On the walk Paulo's hounds bay and jump on us and push against our legs. I shout to them, trying to hide my fear, and the girls shriek, but Rosie kicks them hard and they stop.

Rosie and I run back and forth to the kitchen, infuriating Santiago with our demands for pans of hot water. The four of us crowd into the big square tub and splash and scrub one another until we are worn down, like deflating tires. Rosie and I say there is no way we are going back out to the bunkhouse now. We borrow hairbrushes and makeup and the Dallas girl lends me a crucifix on a chain to wear to dinner. While I am fastening it she whispers to me: Circle Back, between Muleshoe and Lubbock.

She unbuttons my shirt two buttons lower, and I say I hope the cross will bring me luck. No one is paying enough attention to ask me why I need it.

Marcelo and Leonardo are Paulo's banderilleros, men who play the bull and place barbs with crepe paper streamers in the bull's back, early in the corrida. They both live on the ranch, though Leonardo is talking about buying a small house in the village. He wants to have a family. Paulo says you can depend on Leonardo for anything. Marcelo, on the other hand, is moody and quixotic, but he would throw himself in the path of a steaming bull to save another man's life.

When life is ordinary, Marcelo and Leonardo have a status in Paulo's life not because they are part of his retinue, but because they are themselves. Both of them came to the ranch as boys looking for work, and Paulo saw something in them and gave them their roles in his life. Marcelo, gruff and preening, alternately sour and cheerful, tells great jokes and has a wonderful rough voice. He once went to Portugal with Paulo, and he has a huge repertoire of Portuguese and Spanish songs, especially the mournfully beautiful fado. Sometimes when he sings I feel it like a hand in my chest and I want to throw myself on him and beg him to let me make him happy. Such is the power of fado. Leonardo, a quiet, gentle man, is learning all aspects of ranch work and Paulo says he will one day be in charge of the bulls. He is an accomplished guitarist, completely self-taught from scratchy records.

Paulo sometimes asks them to perform for him in the evening, and they sit in the bar and drink a beer or two together, then play until Paulo dismisses them and goes to bed. At those times, they are like brothers or maybe nephews to Paulo, despite their class differences, and his affection for them is apparent. I have been around them many times, but I always sit to the side quietly. This was how I came to love Marcelo, I suppose; and also from the time I spent with him in the city, where he showed me parts of it I would never have known on my own, like the big dance halls and the shantytowns and the cliffs below rich people's houses where poor families live in caves.

When there are guests—American or Mexican movie stars and businessmen who came to hunt, sometimes glamorous women and sometimes beautiful whores and almost never wives—Paulo's "boys" are part of the hospitality. They are performers and they run errands for everyone. I think this is hard on Marcelo, whose ego is large and conflicted, but not on Leonardo, a placid man who feels fortunate and who is capable of adapting to the changes in his opportunities.

So in this instance, as we all troop into the dining room with its elegant chandeliers and extravagant place settings, I see Marcelo and Leonardo eating in the kitchen. I catch Marcelo's eye as I pass the door, but he ducks his head.

A town official is at the table with his teenage son, and also the matador Lara, the actress, the Americans, Rosie, Felix and me. Paulo's poor cousin Nando has come by bus and he is there, too, and of course Paulo at the head of the table. And Chule, looking miserable but gallant and grateful. He would rather be in the kitchen with the boys and the cook, as would I. I can imagine Chule passing by the men at the arena, and Paulo tapping Chule on the arm with the stick he used to scratch the javelina and saying, You'll eat with us tonight, son.

Stay clear of the city men and the gringas, now.

A joke, of course, but hard for a serious boy to swallow.

Paulo and Lara sit at opposite ends. Throughout the long and excellent meal, Lara talks to everyone, across the table or down its length. He is a gracious man and Paulo cedes the table to him as the senior person in the room. Chule is sitting across from me and several chairs away. He listens with respect to the anecdotes about admirable men, and the jokes and gossip about the less worthy. He strains to learn something from the talk, though it is frivolous. One of the American women asks if bulls ever survive the fight, and Paulo tells the familiar tale of Civilon, a noble bull in civil-war era Barcelona that was so brave that the crowd demanded he live. Unfortunately, that same night rebel soldiers broke into the pens and slaughtered him. Paulo enjoys the look of distress on the women's faces when he gets to that part; later he'll say to me, They go for it every time.

Lara squeezes a lime over a slice of melon and turns to Chule and asks him how things are going for him.

On Friday I go to Torreon, Chule says. A long ride.

Good, good, Lara says. I'm certain we will see more of you next year.

Chule doesn't know to let it go. With a shrug he says, My kills.

Paulo rings a bell to call for the table to be cleared.

Lara speaks gently to Chule. I saw one of your novilladas. You had bad luck with the bulls. But don't worry, we all have our stories. I fought nine novilladas in a row years ago, and never cut an ear!

Paulo, who is famous for his cool and precise kills, says,

Chule is a good boy. He won't get in a hurry, like so many of these snotty youngsters who think they can kneel in the dust and spite the bull, like that hippie, Cordobes. They think they will be famous because they mock death.

There is a murmur of agreement at the table. The actress Carla smiles at Paulo and strokes his hand. Nando always has to weigh in, too, as if his kinship makes him expert. It strikes me that he looks like a weasel.

So many things can go wrong, he says.

He had his own try in dusty villages ten, fifteen years ago, and this is the extent of his wisdom, though he has an engineering degree from a Texas university, an American ex-wife and children in Austin, a whole life he didn't have the good sense to hold onto because he wishes he had Paulo's.

Lara says, They don't know what it means to kill cleanly, over the horns and to the hilt.

I am surprised to hear platitudes from the matadors. Maybe it is sociable chit chat, like talk of the weather, but if you have read anything at all about the subject, it is boring. I don't know what I expected. Maybe gossip about other fighters, or a recounting of a great fight. News of a newcomer in Spain, or complaints about the management of the rings.

The visitor from the village toasts Paulo, gracious host, breeder of prize horses and brave toros, rancher and owner of packing plants, employer of most of the men in the village of Tamuin, star of Western movies, but most of all, the keenest, cleanest, most breathtaking of killers.

Felix stands and takes a bow.

Perhaps I will show you all something tomorrow, he says, as I did last year, when I was so brave with the muleta, wiggling my tail instead of the cloth, all for your amusement!

Paulo rises and we all leave the room. Chule manages to be last and disappears through the kitchen. Lara begins singing a country song as we make our way to the bar, on the walkway to the gate. The bar is made up like a saloon in an old Colorado mining town, with a long mirror and bar hauled all the way from somewhere north of Denver. Marcelo and Leonardo come in and stand at the far corner. Leonardo begins to strum the twelve-string guitar, and Marcelo sings with his eyes closed and his head thrown back. Rosie told me once that a man from Mexico heard Marcelo sing and offered to help him get a recording contract, but Marcelo was insulted; only the maricons, the queer ones, go for that, he said.

I slip out and go back to the house and up to the library.

Soon after I came to the ranch I admired Paulo's eclectic, fascinating collection, but I also said it was chaotic and I didn't see how he could stand it. How did he find anything? He challenged me to organize it, and I did. I spent a month on it, handling every book and rearranging the shelves by categories. Botany, archeology and anthropology, and of course so many books about animals, especially of Africa. Books about Hitler and guns and war. A complete collection of Olympia Press pornography, and all of Hemingway. Dozens of his mother's old art books, and heaps of paperbacks left behind by guests. And of course everything about bullfighting, in Spanish, Portuguese, and English. I worked my way through every book on the subject. Sometimes I was in the library all night, the door shut and the air conditioner on high. I found a sheaf of letter paper in a drawer and I began to write as a nightly habit, sitting on the floor, leaning against the shelves; often I wrote all night, until I heard Santiago coming in to start breakfast. I tried to reconstruct conversations I had heard during my time in Mexico City, and to describe the things I had seen at the ranch.

Paulo found me like that one night, and I confessed my dream of being a writer, like Jane Bowles or Katherine Anne Porter. Dreams are silly, he said. The only way to achieve anything is to begin to do it. The next day he had someone bring up a discarded typewriter and a stand, and a brand new box of paper.

I stay in the library for an hour or so until I can imagine myself sleeping. I take the crucifix from around my neck and hang it on the girls' doorknob. From the top of the stairs, near Paulo's door, I can hear the sounds of his voice and Carla's. I slip down the stairs. Awful music, some old crooner on a scratchy record, is coming from the parlor where the bear stands, and I hear the laughter of women and the low murmur of men's voices. I wonder who is in there; I think I hear Ofelia.

A wind is up and the air is heavily humid. I make my way along the walk, anxious as always because of the dogs. They assail me right away. I know they wouldn't hurt me, but their loud baying makes my pulse race, and they crowd me.

At the gate they are still at me. I put my hand on the latch as they push against me, and then, for no reason I could state, I turn and let them shove their noses along my thighs and into my crotch. Then the gate opens, and Milo kicks at the dogs and pulls me through.

Not long after I get into bed it rains hard for a while, then abruptly stops. Rosie bursts into the room drunk. She crawls into bed and cuddles up to me to get warm. Later I think I hear Felix at the door. I think he opens the door and says my name, but he sees that Rosie is there and he goes away. In the morning I think that I might have dreamed it. He didn't really speak to me the whole evening. And why would he need to leave the house if he wanted sex or company or a place to sleep?

People from other ranches and a few officials from the village have arrived for the tienta. There is a photographer and a boy lugging his equipment. Plenty of amateurs would have liked to attend, but Paulo allows little fooling around. To some, this is a game, a sport, but he is raising brave bulls, and the tienta, their testing, is serious business. As host, he has to balance the social aspects of the occasion with the real purpose of the work.

A brave bull leads a lovely life until he is led into the ring. The work of the ranch is to assure that he is handsome, strong, and brave. The stud bull has a harem, and the cows must not be timid creatures, or, it is believed, the progeny will be disappointing and even shameful. So there is the testing. The cows are lanced and caped (they can be very fast) and if they perform well they are chosen for breeding; if not, they are someone's meat. The young bulls, too, are driven into the small ring where they face cowboys on horseback; ideally, a brave bull never meets a man on foot, and certainly not one with a cape. If they run from a lancing instead of charging the horse, they are sorry livestock. If they are lively and fierce, they go back to the pasture and the good life, until it is their time.

The work begins very early in the morning, before the party goers are well awake. We sit on the couches drinking coffee and hot chocolate and passing around bottles of aspirin. Felix and Nando both have hangovers, and the stewardesses simply looked tired. Rosie is the last to appear. We are perfectly happy in our companionable misery, until Ofelia click clacks up the stairs and makes her noisy way down the hall. As she passes me she says, We missed you last night.

We all watch her progress into the kitchen, her ass rolling back and forth, her jeans so tight the cloth disappears into her crack. One of the stewardesses grabs my arm. What was that about? she wants to know and the other one says, She's just a maid.

She's Paulo's secretary, I say. She was a receptionist at his hotel in Valles, and he trained her to handle money and correspondence. She's full of herself around strangers. She thinks she's something because she knows his business. It's a very small world here.

She fucked that weenie guy from town, one of the stewardesses remembers now.

You should get her in trouble, they say. She was awful snotty to you.

Rosie and I exchange a look and I tell them Paulo wouldn't care.

What the hell, I think. I tell them how, when I first came, she worked late one night and stayed over at the ranch. After supper she suggested to Paulo that we all go to bed together, she would show me some things. I wouldn't do it, I went off to bed and Paulo went to bed and I guess it humiliated her. She thinks I think I am better than her, which I do, but only because I have no one else to look down on.

Eww, the stewardesses say together. She's so ugly.

Nando, moving closer to them, says, I love women. I love sex. I love the ranch. He makes all of us laugh.

About eleven Paulo sends someone to get us and we watch the cowboys and then the boys with the capes—Marcelo, Leonardo, and Chule. The teenager from the village asks to go into the ring, but his father tells him it's not time. There will be the smaller calves in the late afternoon.

I can't eat lunch. I have said nothing to anyone since I worked with Chule, but I have decided I will go into the ring. I ask Paulo if I can stand down by the barrier, to be closer to the action. The barrier runs around the ring to keep the livestock from the stands, and there are other, shorter barriers in front of that one, where the men can wait or escape. In a bullfight you often see bulls slam against the barriers, and once I saw one jump it and go right into the stands.

Paulo dismisses me with a wave of his hand, saying, Don't get in the way, and I take that as grudging permission. As soon as we get to the ring, I slip down beside Leonardo, who greets me with a smile. I wish I ever liked a man as tender as he is.

The work goes well, which is to say that Paulo's bulls and cows and calves and men are all what they should be, and after a few hours, girls from the house bring us ice water and there is a break. Then the smaller calves are brought. Felix has his turn and makes much of his own ungainliness, deliberate, I now see, for the fun of it. Nando has been practicing, and he tries out elaborate, inappropriate cape work until Paulo tells him to stop. The teenager is graceless but adequate with a smaller calf, and looks broken-hearted when Paulo gestures for him to finish up. I am still behind the barrier near Leonardo and now Chule. Chule drapes his cape over the barrier near me and my heart lofts in gratitude. Across the ring I catch Marcelo's eye and he glares at me. He goes out with a calf, perfunctory now with the easiness of it, and then Paulo calls out, This one is last.

It is a little animal, more like a goat than a cow, with immature horns and a furious twitchy tail. I grab Chule's cape and run into the ring, almost meeting Marcelo in the middle. He passes the calf and hisses at me to get out. There is a minor clamor in the stands, but I hear Paulo say, It's well enough.

Chule has played the cow on the other side of the ring, and Marcelo has turned his back to the ring and gone behind the boards. The little cow tosses her head and turns, looking this way and that. Behind me, I hear Leonardo call, Go toward the center, and I do. I hold the cape out and high, as if it were Chule coming toward me. The cow sees the lure and comes for it. I don't have time to be afraid, though I will remember those moments afterwards in slow motion, as if I had all the time in the world to turn and run.

I am lucky. The cow is a good girl, straight and fast, thoroughly annoyed, and not afraid. She behaves the way she is meant to behave, and that makes my simple pass the right one to let her by. As I lift my cape behind her, I know my pass has not been beautiful, but look at me: I stand my ground and look for Paulo, finding only the glare of the sun.

The animal skids to a stop behind me, looks around, and decides to charge again. I know this because this is what a good calf does in the ring. It is my place to turn, too, and pass her again, but I am still, as if my clock has stopped. Someone calls out to me and I turn quickly and hold out the cape.

The cow slips by me so close I see the ridge of her back. She runs toward the barrier where Leonardo and Chule are calling to her. I drop the cape. I hear the matador Lara call out, in clear English, Now run! and I do, while behind me the young men work the cow to an exit.

I ride back in a jeep with Leonardo, Chule, Rosie and the actress. They clap me on the back and tell me I am a brave chihuahua. I go straight to the bunkhouse and lock myself in my room. Nobody comes for me for dinner. I am afraid I have embarrassed Paulo and myself. Suddenly I ache with exhaustion, and I go to sleep.

I wake up in the middle of the night starving. I figure I will startle the dogs and make a terrible racket, but they have been moved away from the house, and everything is quiet. It is a dark night, but I have the flashlight.

I make my way to the kitchen, close the door, and make scrambled eggs and toast. I carry my plate and a Coke into the library, close the door, and sit down behind the desk. I eat quickly, almost thrilling to the taste of the food and the feel of it in my stomach. I have slept six or seven hours and I know I won't sleep again. I'll have to find something to read.

I push my plate aside and that is when I notice a large manila envelope on the desk. I am looking at it from the open end, and I see that it is stuffed with glossy 8 x 10 photographs. I pull them out.

They are from Paulo's African trips. There are dozens of photographs of Paulo: alone, with his girlfriend, his guns, his dead game, his guides and bearers. I pick up a picture so odd I think it has to be a hoax. A very tall Masai is holding his spear and smiling into the camera. Along his leg is what appears to be an extraordinarily long penis looped in a knot.

I jump when the door is flung open. There stands Paulo naked.

Huh, huh, torera! he says. He grins in the boyish way he sometimes does. Then he sees the photographs and takes the one of the Masai from my hand. Quite a fellow, he says.

Is it real?

It? Yes, all fifteen inches of it.

I try to tidy the stack of pictures and put them back in the envelope, but Paulo has sat down on the rug and he motions for me to come sit down with him.

The photographer said he got several shots of you. The one I want is when you dropped the cape.

Ouch, I say.

Paulo stands up. You lifted your left leg, like this—

He demonstrates, his penis dangling.

—and propped it against your other knee like a stork.

I didn't!

The photograph will prove it.

I try to laugh. I don't want him to say anything else, since he isn't going to say I was good at it. So I ask, Did Carla like it in Africa? She's so pretty in the photographs.

He takes one of the pictures from the desk and studies it for a moment, then turns to me and says, Everybody wants. Carla wants to get married; she would love the press. Ofelia wants me to give her a job in my office in Mexico. Santiago wants to cook in the hotel. Leonardo wants a house in the village, and Marcelo, poor sucker, wants to be Chule, starting out as a young torero. The American girls want to fuck a bullfighter. My Kikuyu guide wanted to come back to Mexico with me. And then there's you. What do you want, nena?

I'm surprised. He never asks me about myself. He doesn't know where I grew up, or where I started college, or whether I have family. He doesn't have any curiosity about women, maybe not about people in general. He saw me by the pool at his hotel in Valles and took me back to his ranch like something he bought at Sears.

I want an answer. Don't go digging around for something clever. Just tell me what you want.

I want to see things, Paulo. I want to remember things. And one day I'll write about them. Maybe I'll write about you.

He claps his hands together once. Come on. I'm going to get dressed. I'll show you things right now. You won't have to write them down to remember.

What do you mean? What about Carla? It's the middle of the night.

She's asleep and I know what time it is. Wait right here, chica. We'll take a ride.

He puts a rifle and a battery-powered spotlight in the Land Rover and we take off into the night. We race along the drive to the runway, turn left and speed to the end of it. He drives for a couple of minutes straight into darkness. I can't make out anything at all. It's like falling into a well. Then he pulls to a stop and turns on the light. He sweeps the light from left to right.

There! See the deer?

I see the other-worldly shine of animal eyes. He drives on, stops, drives and stops. Each time I see more. Small creatures scuttle across our path. Others freeze, blinded by the light. With each stop we seem to be closer to the edge of the world, surrounded by more and more animals, as if they are gathering around us. I know there are wild cats out here, and I am afraid. How quickly could Paulo fire his gun? And what if something leaped on him first? Or on me?

He stops again, and turns out the light. Instantly we are in complete blackness, and I reach out frantically and grasp his arm.

He says, If you want to see, you have to look. You can learn to see. The animals are looking at you.

I feel rather than see the gesture of his arm, his sweep of the possibilities out there. I am trembling.

He pulls me toward him, and clambers out of the jeep. I stumble against him.

He pulls me away from the vehicle. I reach behind me with my hand, just able to brush it with my fingers and relieved to know I can. I hear him unzip his pants and the sound of his piss hitting the dirt. He steps farther away from me.

Paulo!

He isn't far. He says, You surprised me today. You have never surprised me before, you know.

I don't know why I thought I could do it.

The smallest calf.

I know, I know, it was nothing.

If I left you out here—

Don't say that, please.

What would you do?

I can hardly keep from crying. I say, I'd choose a direction I thought was the house, and I would put one foot in front of the other.

He steps close to me again, and relief floods me. He likes to tease, but he has never been cruel to me.

Maybe I will take you to Africa next year. Would you like that? To go on safari? Could you tear yourself away from your busy life? Would you come along, and take notes?

He is standing inches from me but not touching me. I sense creatures around us. I hear their scratchy noises and their snuffling.

He says, I could find the Masai again. I could introduce you to him.

I force a small laugh.

What do you think he says when he spreads the legs of a woman?

What could he say? How could he do that?

He whispers: He says, I'll just put the head in.

I start to laugh and I can't stop. I laugh myself into a hiccuping fit. Paulo slides his arm under my shirt and pats my back. I can't stop laughing. My whole body shakes. I turn and put my palms against the jeep, cawing and snorting. He hits me again, but I can't stop, and then he hits me harder, first on my shoulder, then on the side of my face. He would knock me down except for my arms extended, my hands flat against the side of the jeep, my feet planted on solid ground.

Swim

They met Baby the day they got off the ferry looking like the hick tourists they were. The crowd from the boat flowed around them while they dawdled at the end of the quay. They weren't even on the island they thought they were, and they had no idea what to do next.

Look at us, a couple of ducks at a dog show, Walker said.

I ain't getting back on a boat for days, Bony said. I'm a soldier not a seaman.

Walker slapped Bony's shoulder.

Wasn't this your idea?

He shrugged one shoulder to hitch up the strap of his duffel bag.

I'm starved, Bony said.

The harbor was behind them and in front of them was a maze of white-washed buildings piled up like kids' blocks. Off to the right there were tables shaded by a big blue tarp. A man with a white cloth tucked in his waistband was serving customers from a large tray. Walker pointed at them.

How about over there?

I'm not picky, Bony said.

All of a sudden there was a young skinny woman in a hot pink shift beside them.

You don't want to do that.

They stared at her.

The thing is, as soon as they see a boat pulling in, they switch menus and double their prices. You have to get out of sight of water. Are you day-trippers?

Do what? Bony said.

When I got here three weeks ago, there were crowds pouring in and out all day. Not so many now. You came at the right time.

Walker shaded his eyes and assessed the hills.

This ain't Santorini, huh?

The woman pointed to the crones lined up like ravens on a roof. They were shouting at a handful of tourists.

They will rent you rooms. If you don't mind four in a room, you can get a bed for a quarter. For a few bucks, you could share a room, just the two of you.

Like the barracks, Bony said.

I'll check some places I know after we eat.

They turned a few corners and lined up at a window in an alley wall. The café was a three-sided closet. In the back there were grills over stone cooking pits.

The woman said, Your treat, okay?

She ordered and Bony paid.

Oh Baby, he said after his first bite. You are off to a good start.

They ate scraped morsels of crackled lamb on folded flat

bread with tomatoes, cucumbers, a tart white sauce. They sat on a low wall, leaning forward to let the sandwiches drip.

They introduced themselves. Walker was the taller man, with broad shoulders and a wide firm chin. Bony had the same chin on a smaller face. He was small in the hips like a teenage boy. They were cousins, sons of brothers.

Hodell, Walker said. Rhymes with yodel. Everyone remembers that.

They were on leave from an army base in Germany. Their hair was cut close and their clothes were clean and crisp.

We're from Lawton, Oklahoma. You probably don't know where that is.

Guess again. My mother was born in Chickasha. I was born in Wichita Falls.

Oh Baby, Bony said. I'd never take you for a Texan. What's your name?

Baby's good, she said. Y'all can call me that.

They followed her through the maze out onto a square.

Wait here.

Walker lit a cigarette and they watched a group of girls swarm through the square in tight formation. The girls wore short dresses or tank tops and bell-bottom pants. They wore long earrings and jangly bracelets. They looked around as they walked—flitty, pretty girls. They saw the men, but with the flickering attention of fireflies.

Man, I could go for some of that, Walker said.

Bony was thinking about something else. Baby looked a lot like his sister, Kell.

You think she's a whore? he said.

The room was the interior of a windmill near the town beach, farther on from the harbor, beyond the square. There were two beds, a table and one wooden chair, a single bare bulb in the ceiling. There were big jugs of water and a white enamel pan. Two towels. The bathroom was an outhouse a few steps outside a door. There was no running water.

Baby stood in the doorway while they looked around.

Scenic, Walker said.

Bony threw his bag down on the end of the bed away from the door. Dibs, he said.

Baby took their money to pay three nights.

Hey, you got a friend? Walker asked.

She laughed.

It's not all that friendly a place. I do have a roommate, Dafne. She's German. I can ask.

Great, Bony said, though German girls scared him.

After she was gone, the men sat on the beds. There wasn't much give. Thin mattresses were laid on low rough wood platforms and covered in coarse white sheets and multi-colored woven spreads. The pillows were terrible sacks of stuffing, but the men were used to that. They stretched out and listened to the whap of the paddles turning above them. They had left Athens before dawn.

The room was light and cool, with four open windows high in the walls. Bony stood up and looked out of one.

This beats Berlin, he said.

They had gone to Berlin one weekend in March and had a terrible time.

Walker dumped his duffel bag out on his bed.

Let's go swim. We are on a gee-dee island.

So do you?

Do I what?

Think she's out for something.

Sure she is, Bony. But that don't make her a prostitute. Did you see her wolf down lunch? She was hungry. She earned it. If she was hot to trot, she wouldn't have got us a double room, would she? She'd have split us up and took her pick.

Bony thought it over.

Maybe we're just lucky. That she's friendly and all.

He didn't like judging people. In the Army you did what you were told to do. It took a load off him not to think so much.

Walker stripped and pulled on his swim trunks. Bony changed, too. It was plenty warm, but his pale legs felt pimply and cold. They both put on T shirts and ugly sandals they had bought in Athens. They picked up their towels.

Bony waited. Walker was thinking. Walker was a year older; in a week he would be twenty-one. He had been born the day the Japs surrendered. Bony figured that was why Walker was more serious. Bony looked to him a lot for explanations.

Did you see those girls in the square, Bony? You see yourself sidling up to one of them? Shoot. We're out of our league on this candy-ass island.

You don't know what you'll find when you go out to see the world, Bony said. They both laughed, because it was just plain true.

They found their way to the beach. Along the way, Bony got to thinking.

What are they like, the ones around the base?

It was easy, one of the first things you heard when you arrived. You get a pass, walk off the base, turn right or left or go straight ahead. The whores find you. You go in a bar, or maybe you don't even do that. You don't have to know anything.

Walker said, You think I'd tell you?

Both men were Hardshell Primitive Baptists. They had grown up in families who didn't drink, dance, play cards, curse or chase women. Still, you couldn't be in the Army and not learn a few new things. They liked a beer once in a while, and poker for low stakes, and rock and roll. But women? When they left Lawton, all they had known were girls.

Bony still wrote to his high school girlfriend, Candace, who was in Alva studying to be a nurse. He had touched her breasts once under her shirt and she told her mother. He caught hell from all sides, but it blew over. They didn't have any plans. Walker had never been attached. He had about decided to be an Army man for the long haul.

The beach was nothing to write home about, but the sea was turquoise. They splashed around and declared the water alone was worth the trip. Walker swam way out past everyone and back, then cut across and swam parallel to the beach. Mostly he did a steady strong crawl, even and pure as a machine. A girl sat up and watched him a while, then lay down.

When Walker got back to their towels, Bony was asleep. Walker nudged Bony's shin.

Let's walk around. I like to know where I am.

They found free public showers on a side street off the square, then went to the room to change clothes.

It's a pretty place, Walker said. Don't seem exactly real, though, does it?

Do you ever wonder what you would be like if you'd been born someplace else?

No. I don't ask myself dumb-ass questions, Bony.

They stood around the square a while but there was no sign of Baby among the crowd of tourists. It was hot and most people had bared as much skin as they could. Walker and Bony picked out the Scandinavians, who walked with long strides and were tall, and the French, who were small and noisy.

A girl in a bikini brushed right by Walker. He could smell the suntan lotion on her skin. He could smell her hair. He said, Lord-ee.

The outdoor cafés were getting crowded. It was almost dark. They went to the café with the blue tarpaulin, over by the harbor, and found a free table.

You boys have the right idea, the waiter said cheerfully. Eat with Greeks. We cook one hundred percent Greek!

He gestured to a nearby table. It was crowded with black-haired men. On the other side of those men was a family with two neatly dressed little boys.

Where are the Greek girls? Walker asked.

Home with their mothers! The waiter laughed. He said, We got good meatballs. Americans, they like meatballs.

We get the same prices as them? Walker asked, gesturing to the Greek customers.

The waiter made a great show of wounded astonishment.

We got best food, best prices for everybody. You go around and check, you come back here!

They ordered lemonades. The waiter shook his head as if it were a sad mistake.

Everybody's got advice, Bony said. It was nice. In Berlin even the hotel clerk had been unhelpful.

The lemonades came; grassy bits floated on top. The men

scooted their chairs so they could lean against the wall. Walker picked the specks out of his drink with the straw.

A lot of tourists had appeared almost at once. Walker said, What's going on, do you think?

It's a danged parade, Bony said. He waved at the waiter and ordered a plate of meatballs. It came on a plate in a pool of oil, with a heap of bread. They watched the stream of tourists while they ate hurriedly, their heads low, force of habit.

A pelican waddled right by them.

Will you look at that? Walker said.

Bony said, Gee, I wish I'd ordered fish.

One of the men at the neighboring table stuck his foot out and jostled the pelican. The bird raised its broad wings and scuttled by. Some tourists nearby laughed, stepping back to make room. One of the kids at the nearby table shrieked. Walker said, How often do you think they have to wind him up?

The bird or the boy? Bony said.

Here you are! Baby said when she caught up with them.

We ate without you, Bony said.

I had that big lunch.

She plucked a leftover piece of bread and swiped it through the meatball grease and ate it quickly.

She led them to a part of town where balconies hung out over the water. Every bar was playing whining Greek music. They came to a small place with a low doorway and went inside. They took seats near the balcony along a cool plastered wall that felt good against their backs.

This place is owned by a couple of Canadians, Baby said. In an hour it will be packed.

Over a speaker on the wall near them they heard Bobby Darin singing "Mack the Knife." They ordered beer and Baby asked for a plate of olives and cheese, and water with lemon. The music changed. The Animals, Baby said. I met them on Mallorca, on this little beach not far from Palma. Some of them, anyway. The band broke up, you know.

What were they like? Bony said. He wasn't sure who The Animals were, but he recognized the music. *Don't let me be misunderstood.*

Laid back and rowdy at the same time. Just hanging out, but horsing around. They weren't cruising for girls. I guess they could have had them if they'd put out the word.

Like us, Walker said, and laughed.

Soon the place had filled up and the music was louder. People danced, waving their arms, twisting their shoulders and hips.

Hey! Over here! Baby called, waving her arm. A plump pretty girl started toward them. She looked young, maybe just out of high school. She had a short ponytail, pale and silky.

Baby introduced them.

Dafne crawled over Walker and squeezed in next to Baby. Bony was on Baby's other side. Dafne leaned across Baby and squeezed Bony's arm.

Little but hard, she said.

Vodka, she told the waiter. Then I'll switch to ouzo.

Baby said she would have a beer after all; they drank two rounds. They tried Dafne's ouzo and said it was vile. Dafne said it was time to dance. She pushed Walker to get out and tugged at his arm.

I don't think so, he said.

She shrugged and grabbed Baby's hand.

The women danced, laughing and shaking. Dafne had large breasts, unbound under a thin tank top. You couldn't help looking.

Dafne yelled, What's keeping you? She gave them a hard look. A dare.

Bony got up first. He had two left feet. He danced with Baby by standing in place and pumping his arms while she dipped and whirled. At first he looked around to see what other guys were doing, but it was easier not to know. Walker and Dafne were belly to belly, slowed-down and busy right around the hips. A second song ended and they all plopped on the bench and drained the last drops from bottles and glasses. Walker lit a cigarette and offered his pack around.

Dafne took three cigarettes and threw them in her bag. She spotted someone across the room and waved furiously.

Gotta go, she said. She crawled over Walker and pushed her way past dancers. In a minute they saw her at the door with a guy in cut-offs and no shirt.

I have that effect on so many girls, Walker said.

They left and Baby led them to the house where she was staying. The owner's family lived downstairs. Shhh, Baby said at the bottom of the stone steps.

They climbed to a narrow half-enclosed stucco porch where two beds fit in close together. Through a doorway they could see four empty beds in the next room. Off the porch was the outhouse.

Baby motioned for them to sit on the bed that was against the outside wall. She sat across from them, kicked off her shoes, stretched out her legs across the narrow space, and propped her feet on Bony's knees. He touched a little toe.

This little piggy, he said, and stopped. The ends of her toes and the pads of her feet were streaked with stringy scabs and scars, as if they had been finely, shallowly sliced. He put his hands around her feet, his thumbs against the arches.

She moved a pillow behind her and leaned against it.

You don't really seem the Greek island types.

Bony wants to see the world, Walker said. We go here and there when we can.

I saw pictures of Santorini, Bony said. It looked so pretty and clean.

Walker said, Why are you here?

My boyfriend's best friend is a Greek immigrant. Nemo. He has an Italian wife, Gina, two little kids. We hang out with them on Sundays.

I asked Nemo about Greece and he told me how beautiful the barren hills and the beaches are. The white houses and the light. He made Greece sound so poetic, he made me want to come see for myself. I saved my money. One day I asked Gina if she had gone to Greece with Nemo, and she told me this bitter story.

They were getting married. A big Italian wedding. So she's got on her wedding dress and a telegram arrives. Her mother brings it in and they read it together. Nemo had sent it just before he got on the plane to Greece. It's too soon, it said.

He spent a year here, on this island. When he got back, he heard right away that Gina had had a baby boy while he was gone. So they got married.

Wow, Walker said. Would you call that a happy ending?

Not happy. Satisfactory. She was thirty-five years old with a baby. It worked out, but she didn't forget. She told me, didn't she? And she also told me: You need to leave Dante. He's too old for you. He drinks too much.

Dante? Walker said.

He was born in Rome but he's American now. He doesn't want to be Italian, but he's got the looks. The first time she saw him, my girlfriend said: He's got a statue's head. He calls himself Don, when he has that beautiful name. My friends and I call him "the Count." Once when he was drunk, he started telling me about his father, who is a retired diplomat. If I go to Rome, maybe I'll try to find him.

She laughed. I'll say, Hi, I'm your American son's mistress. What do you think he'll say to that?

Neither of the men answered. They had never known a count, a diplomat, or a mistress.

The music from the bars was far away and faint. A few people walked by in the alley below. Baby got up and squeezed between Bony and Walker.

The day I left, Don said to call him when I was ready to come home. So superior. He figured I'd spend all my money and get stuck.

Have you?

Not quite. It's cheap here if you're careful. She shrugged. No reason to stay, no reason to go.

Walker said, I like to swim better than almost anything, but I'd get bored here. I might be bored tomorrow.

I am so bored, Baby said. She laughed.

She laid her head on Walker's lap and her legs across Bony's thighs. They stayed like that, not talking, until two girls came up the stairs, followed by Dafne.

The men clambered to their feet. They nodded at the girls as they went past, giggling.

Dafne said, Wait, wait.

She rummaged in her big bag and found a ball of something in paper.

Try a little of this.

She unwrapped the ball. It was the color of mud, a little smaller than a golf ball. She got a knife out of her bag.

Sit down! she said in a low, urgent voice. I need one of your cigarettes.

She sat on her bed and slit the cigarette open and scraped the ball with the knife.

Walker and Bony shifted their weight, scuffing the floor with their shoes.

Baby said, You don't want to get high?

Bony said, Not me.

Walker said, We're outta here.

Dafne laughed and said, We could do something else! I have lots of ideas.

They went down the steps, followed by Baby. They heard Dafne still laughing.

Baby said, How would she know if she didn't ask? It's how she makes her way here. It's hash, not a bomb. Here you are right in a nest of cosmopolitan tourists out for a good time. That's where you are.

I get that, Walker said.

In the alley, he said, She talks a lot. Rock stars. Royalty.

He yawned.

Bony said, Did you see her eat that greasy bread?

Later he read, lying on his stomach, his head at the end of the bed, where the weak light was best. He had a pocket sized edition of the New Testament; he carried it everywhere and read at night before bed. He read straight through, then started over again. He had read it so many times he didn't stop to think what he was reading. He was in Luke now.

He wondered what Baby read or did or thought about at night before she slept. He had noticed she had a light wrinkle right between her eyes, the kind you get from worrying.

Baby found them on the beach late the next morning. She said, You have to see the island farther in, guys. Better beaches.

They went up to the square. A rattling sputtering bus was just coming to a stop. Half a dozen people climbed out and they got on.

More people got on than had got off. Everyone carried towels and bags. It was hot in the bus but most of the windows didn't work. There was a smell of stale cigarette smoke and sweat. The thin dirty leather of the seats was worn and torn in places. They bounced and jolted while the driver sang mournful songs.

The driver thinks he's Johnny Mathis, Walker said. *The chances are your chances are awfully good.*

I wonder what he thinks of all of us, Baby said.

They made a stop after a few kilometers, alongside some dry fields. Nobody got off. The driver ate a fig, the juice dripping down his chin. Baby leaned against Walker with her eyes closed. After ten minutes, in which nothing happened to explain the stop, the bus lurched forward again.

Bony sat behind Baby and Walker. He worked on his

window until it creaked open. Riders around him applauded.

The road climbed barren hills circuitously until the harbor and the village lay below them. They passed large stone circles. At one curve, Bony said, I wish I had a picture of that.

In the haze they could see the brown extremities of other islands. The earth was dry and rocky, latticed here and there with low walls. They saw a skinny man high on the skeleton of a windmill, attaching a yellowed sail. Finally, the bus heaved over the crest of a hill and a beach came into sight, a wide curve of sand against the huge expanse of green sea. They climbed down the hill below the bus and ran crazily along the sand, whipping their towels above their heads, shouting and laughing. Passengers from the bus went by them and found places to settle on the sand.

Baby threw her stuff down under an olive tree, high away from the water, and pulled off her shift. She was wearing a dark blue bikini. Her breasts and stomach were so flat she was like a plank. She flopped down and rummaged in her bag, a large pocket of woven wool with a flap and a long strap. She took out a bottle of sun lotion and, over their mild protests, she rubbed Bony's back and shoulders, and then Walker's.

Walker said, Gimme that.

He squeezed out lotion on Bony's hands and then his own. With a jerk of his head, he assigned Baby's legs to Bony. He took her arms and back.

Bony massaged cream into the soles of her feet.

They lay down, their heads close together, their bodies out like spokes.

Dafne liked you, Baby told Walker.

Get out.

The guys here. Either they ignore you completely or they expect you to put out.

I don't think like that.

See? That's the deal.

Walker sat up. So let me get this straight. We walk off the ferry and you know instantly we're not wild guys.

I guessed it.

Shy guys. Queers, maybe. Dopes.

Nice guys, Baby said. Are you telling me you're not?

Walker got up and ran down the beach and swam vigorously toward the horizon.

He's a devil in the water, Baby said. She was standing, shading her eyes.

Bony said, Oklahoma 1963 high school state champion in free-style.

Baby waved her arms until Walker saw her. He was seventy, eighty yards out, bobbing effortlessly. He waved back. Bony said, Let's go. He swam out as Walker swam in and they slapped hands. Baby went in waist-deep water, then timidly bounced along until the water covered her shoulders.

Walker came close.

Don't you know how to swim?

I had lessons as a kid. But the ocean is intimidating. It's never still. Off Mallorca there were sea-urchins. Eric Burdon stepped on one on a rock.

Can you float?

She made a slight jump into deeper water, where Walker was standing, and lay on her back and arched. Her legs sank and she kicked languidly. She smiled at Walker. He said, If you can float, you can swim. The water's calm here. Go on. Swim.

She looked stricken.

Stay right by me?

She swam: a comical combination of side stroke, scissor kick, breast stroke, with interims of floating. She never put her face in the water. She made a little progress, then turned and clumsily made her way back to shallow water.

I give you a C minus, Walker said. Not quite passing. You wouldn't drown in a backyard pool but that's about as far as you should get from land.

Gee thanks. Didn't I tell you?

I'm going to teach you a proper stroke. What are you afraid of? Getting your hair wet?

I don't like to put my face down. My eyes sting. Sometimes I panic.

Let's start with your float. It's just a few tiny steps to backstroke.

He put his arm lightly under her as she lay on her back. He said, Now, pedal. Like a bike. See? Flutter your arms.

He pressed his arm against her back and moved her hand in and out. He stepped away.

Now pull your arms over your head, one at a time, just like the regular crawl upside down.

She did the strokes and moved a few yards. Then a wave came in and she got a face full of water. She flipped onto her belly and dog-paddled her way back to shallow water. Walker said, You need practice. Confidence. The water's neutral, Baby. It doesn't care that you're there.

When they came out of the water, Bony had their towels. Walker patted Baby's back and tucked her hair behind her ears.

She patted his scruffy chin. She said, You're going to get a beard here.

A boy appeared, selling orange melons. They bought two. The boy plunged his knife into them and they cracked open like eggs. They ate the sweet melons right down to the rinds and drank water from the bottles they had brought. Then they sank down in the shade of the trees. More people had come while they were swimming. The beach was littered with bodies broiling in the sun.

The hike back to the bus was hard and they didn't try to talk. Bony took the front seat in the bus and Baby sat down beside him. They picked up more tired, sunburned tourists. In a while they came over a hill and saw the town below.

Bony said, I'm so hungry I could gnaw your arm off.

Baby lifted her arm and Bony put his mouth on it. His head bumped her chest. She laughed and he pulled back, embarrassed.

The public showers were an enclosure off an alley with two spigots, some pans, and a couple of showerheads with weak pressure. The water was cool. She asked Bony if he would rinse her hair. She filled a basin and handed it to him. She bent over, rubbing her hands in her hair.

When she stood up she whipped her head like a wet dog. Bony thought maybe Candace would be jealous if she knew he had poured water over a girl's head on a Greek island. It sounded romantic, but it wasn't.

Did you notice the scabs and scars on her feet? he asked Walker when they left her.

Who knows where she walks? She's ungodly nuts.

You think only the ungodly feel pain and bear scars?

Whoa! Listen to the preacher talk. I think we got two more nights to go and you'll never see her again. God can love one and not another, Bony. So can I.

Heretic! Bony muttered. But in his heart he knew everyone wasn't saved.

That evening, while they were eating in the square, Baby and Dafne found them and pulled up chairs. They were cheerful and fresh scrubbed, in jeans and T shirts.

Order something, Walker said. Really. Eat up.

But there were scraps of fish, macaroni, tomatoes, bread. The girls cleaned up the platters, eating with their hands. Let's have dessert, Bony said.

Baby ordered pastries that were like donut holes soaked in honey—sweet and gooey but light—that came on a big platter. They ate with their fingers, making a mess. Dafne took Walker's hand and licked two fingers. He blinked at her, as if she had said something in a foreign language.

They went onto the beach where the moonlight made the sand look fragile. They bent at the edge of the water to wash their hands. Walker put his arm around Dafne's waist.

Bony thought, When lust hath conceived, it bringeth forth sin.

What could he say, though? Walker knew the Scripture as well as Bony did.

Right then Baby whispered to Bony, Let's go to church.

The church doors were locked. Bony said, It's okay. These churches make me nervous. The gold, the pictures—we don't worship idols.

I know a place you'd like.

They went through the streets above the town, where there were no lights. Baby took out a small flashlight and shone it on the ground.

She said, We're walking where it's a rough path, so be careful.

He thought he heard an animal in the brush, the skitter of small rocks.

They came to a simple round building with a dark roof. The door was loose on its hinges and squeaked as Baby opened it. When they were inside she shined the light across the walls and the floor. The room was the size of a generous parlor, bare of furniture, with nothing on the walls. Bits of paper and a few bottles were strewn about.

She showed him a spot just out of the moonlight where they could sit facing the door. She picked up a crumpled sweatshirt from the floor, shook it, and put it down for them to sit on. They leaned against the wall and pulled up their knees. She said, It must have been a chapel, but they left nothing in it. You can see there were paintings on the wall over there—

But he couldn't see anything in the illumination from her small flashlight. She clicked the light off. There was a swath of pale moonlight across her face.

I came up here once with girls from my house. One of them had some pot. We smoked and sang Beatles songs. We had all been traveling through the summer. We talked about where we had been, and then we smoked more dope and took off our clothes and danced around. We said, Hey we're witches! We said, There was a time they would have burned us at a stake.

Then one of the girls started crying. She said she wanted to go home. And she did, the next day.

Baby reached over and took Bony's hand.

I felt smug. I've always wanted to be a person who has been places. I came to Europe in May. I've only spent two hundred dollars.

Has it been fun?

I've always been on the go. I hitched a lot, and slept in hostels, and spent days waiting for ferries and buses. I went right through the big cities because they were expensive. I traveled to a place because I'd heard someone mention it, and then as soon as I got there I thought about where to go next. I kept thinking it would be better when I got to this island, but once I settled down I got lonesome. Those girls? That dance? It was like I dreamed it. In two days they were all gone. The expats stay to themselves. The tourists are here a day or two or a week at the most. People get stoned and sleep together and the next day maybe they don't even speak to each other. That happened to me. Not here. In Spain. An Irish guy.

He didn't want to hear about Spain. He said, Why don't you go home?

I don't know where that would be. My boyfriend is in Chicago, but I only lived there a year and we're awful together. I don't have any family to go back to.

She let go of Bony's hand.

Boo hoo, she said. Little orphan. Don't worry, I never cry. I just pick at my feet. We had a little bitty earthquake here one night last week. I thought, my God, I'm going to die in Greece. I sort of liked the idea. I sat up the rest of the night, waiting while the other girls slept right through it. In the morning

my feet were bloody. My boyfriend is always telling me that I
suffer from free-floating anxiety.

Never heard of it.

Ennui?

Nope.

God, I love soldiers, she said, leaning on his shoulder. Salt
of the earth.

That so?

Maybe she was mocking him.

Once I hitchhiked across the whole country to see a soldier
I'd spent two hours with years before. I thought he would
take care of me. Try and guess how that went. Here's what I've
learned about soldiers. They love a free-spirited girl until they
decide she ought to be a better person. They think they can
make it happen if she cooperates.

What about the count? Doesn't he want to marry you and
give you a reason to settle down?

I told you. It's no good. He's forty years old. My mother
would be forty if she were alive. He's with me because I'm
young, and I'm with him because I'm stuck. And we like each
other's friends.

She got up and Bony jumped up beside her. He leaned
against the wall and she stepped away, twisting her shoulders,
jerky.

She said, I want my own damned reasons to be who I am.
Who I become. I want my own schedule for it.

Bony said, My sister, Kell, ran away from Lawton once. She
was fourteen. The police picked her up in Norman five days
later. A waitress had taken her home the night before, and
when Kell was asleep the woman called the police. Kell never

told us about the other nights.

What a bad bad girl! Did she straighten up and fly right?

She flunked out of school. She can't hold a job. My folks tell her what Paul said: —those who do not work shall not eat.

Hey, look at that, Baby said, as if he wasn't saying something here. She shined her light on stuff on the floor. Condoms, cigarette butts. She put her hands on his chest, startling him. The light shined up into his eyes.

Your little sister has her own mind. She just doesn't know how to read it yet. She doesn't know what will make her feel good. Can you guess what makes me feel good, Bony? I bet Walker could guess.

His cheeks flamed. He left the chapel quickly and started onto the path. He took five or six steps and slid down.

Hold on, Bony.

She stepped ahead and shined the light. Follow me, she said, but he couldn't see much better. I'm sorry, she said. Dante says I'm hostile.

His hand stung from the scrape he got when he fell.

We should have come here right off, Walker said. It was morning. He was stretched out on a bed in his swim suit. They had rented a room at the hotel, a half hour walk away from the quay. Hot water. Toilet. A view. They had gone for a swim and had an American breakfast of eggs, bacon, and toast. Coffee, too, not Nescafe.

Bony said, I guess you and that girl had a good time last night.

Walker hooted.

She's a pistol, that one. Listen, Bony, there's something I

need to tell you. I re-upped before we left. I said I would if
they'd send me to Vietnam right away. It's heating up. When I
joined the Army, I thought I might never have a war to fight.
I thought I might spend my whole enlistment driving trucks
full of canned goods and toilet paper around the base.

Bony slapped the bed with the flat of his hand.

Shit, Walker.

You'll go. They'll have to feed the machine.

But you couldn't wait.

Nope. They found me a billet. I'm going in a month.

So there's no use worrying about what's going to happen,
is there?

That's why we joined up. Because our lives aren't our own.
We make their mistakes, not ours.

Walker was right. Bony saw it clear as anything. What a
hick fool he was. He wasn't going to see the world. He was
going to get thrown into it like fuel for a fire. He thought
about Kell again; he hoped she would grow up and be happy.

Walker, I need some advice. I need a little help with
something. I've got an idea and I don't know if it's crazy or not.

I'm listening, Cuz.

Then they went back to town to find Baby.

Baby and Dafne were sitting on the step at their room.

We could hire a fisherman to take us to an island, Baby
said.

Oh we got better than that, Walker said.

The girls showered and then Walker rented beach chairs

and umbrellas below the hotel. They ate hamburgers and fries. They ordered beers and sat on the sand drinking. Bony was the only one who stopped after one.

Don't you go broke, Baby said.

Walker said, We're cleaning out our pockets. We're leaving tomorrow.

Baby sank against her towel. Dafne ran her foot along Walker's calf and said, We better hurry and have more fun, then.

Bony said, There's something we want to talk to you about, Baby. Walker and me. We like you and we're sorry that you're unhappy.

He looked to Walker for help, but Walker was fiddling with Dafne's tit.

Dafne rolled her eyes. She got up and walked away.

Walker said, We have an idea for you to think about.

Baby sat up. Walker took a deep breath.

We want you to go with us back to Germany tomorrow. There are some nice girls on the base, I know you could stay with one of them while you get started.

Started doing what?

Bony said, You're smart. You could work for the Army, on the base. We'd look out for you.

She got up.

You dumb fuck. You didn't listen to a word I've said. I don't want nice guys figuring out how I should live. I don't need somebody to get me a job. I'm doing what I want to do.

She stalked off in the direction of the bathrooms.

Can't say we didn't try, Walker said. He popped another beer.

Everyone was drunk but Bony. Baby came back and acted like nobody had said anything. Dafne and Walker rolled around on their towels. Bony sat in a plastic chair and stared at the sea. He wasn't looking at anything in particular. The sky, the water, mesmerized him. He knew he was a prideful fool and he was sorry he ever met Baby. It is God in His mercy who chooses who is born out of deadness to grace. Let God worry about Baby.

Good God, what is that girl doing? somebody said near them. Bony blinked. A woman walked toward the surf. She called to her friend, Come see what you think.

Bony went down to the water too. Someone yelled, What's up?

Do you think she's okay? a man asked him. Do you know her?

It was surely Baby, at least a hundred yards straight out from the middle of the beach, toward the edge of the earth. She was bobbing in the waves, her head like a piece of flotsam.

Baby! he yelled as loud as he could, but she had gone into a dead man's float.

He yelled again and someone said, I don't think she can hear you, man.

Baby went out into the sea, farther and farther, like a cut-loose float.

Bony ran and shouted at Walker. Walker was half-asleep on the sand, his arm and leg draped over Dafne. He sat up, befuddled, annoyed.

Bony shook his shoulder. You have to do something, he said.

Bony and Walker and Dafne joined others gathering at the edge of the surf. Bony could barely see Baby now.

That dumb little whore, Walker said. Dafne slapped his arm.

You have to go get her, Bony said. He thought he saw a boat farther out, parallel to the shore. A girl on the beach waved her arms back and forth, jumping up and down.

He said to Walker, You're the big dang swimmer.

Walker wiped his face and scratched his head. This is not a good time for this, he said.

Bony thought Baby had to be getting tired out there. He didn't think she was swimming anymore. He looked down at his feet. Was the tide going in or going out? How the hell would he know?

A man waded in and started swimming. His girlfriend screamed, You can't swim worth shit!

Bony went behind Walker and shoved him as hard as he could. Walker stumbled into the water, stooped and splashed himself. I'm not up for this, he said, but he swam, a drunk man trying to sober up.

Bony knew he couldn't swim that far. He knew that if he did get to Baby, he wasn't strong or skilled enough to bring her in. He was no savior, any way you called it.

He ran through the shallows and dove in. He couldn't see Baby far away, placidly adrift, her eyes closed against the world. He couldn't see the clumsy heroes headed toward her, or the boat turning in a big arc to see what the trouble was. He couldn't feel or think, either, or pray. He could just put one arm over, pull, and then the other one, and hope he was going in the right direction.

ABOUT SANDRA SCOFIELD

Sandra Scofield was born and raised in west Texas, lived for 30 years in Southern Oregon, and now divides her time between Missoula, Montana, and Portland, Oregon.

She is the author of seven novels, a memoir, a popular craft book for writers—*The Scene Book*, and most recently, a book of essays about family. Her second craft book, about novel revision, is forthcoming Fall 2017 from Penguin Press. Her many literary awards include an American Book Award and a fiction award from the Texas Institute of Letters; a fiction award from The American Aademy of Arts and Letters, and The American Book Award. She has also received an NEA/ USIA New American Writing Award and fellowships from the National Endowment for the Arts, the Oregon Institute of Letters, and the Oregon Arts Council. Three of her books were NYT Notable Books of the Year. Her most recent book, *Mysteries of Love and Grief*, was runner-up for the Willa Cather Women Writing the West Award (2016).

Scofield has been on the faculty of the University of Iowa Summer Writing Festival for more than twenty years, and is a faculty member of the Pine Manor Solstice Creative Writing Program since 2007. She is also a painter.

sandrajscofield.com

CPSIA information can be obtained
at www.ICGtesting.com
Printed in the USA
FSOW02n0004150517
34184FS